A Western

Christmas

VIVIAN SINCLAIR

Copyright

Published by East Hill Books

Cover design: Vivian Sinclair Books

Cover illustrations credit:
© Marilyn Gould | Dreamstime.com

ISBN-13: 978-1976104985
ISBN-10: 197610498X

To find out about new releases and about other books written by Vivian Sinclair visit her website at VivianSinclairBooks.com or follow her on the Author page at Amazon, Facebook at Vivian Sinclair Books, or on GoodReads.com

Maitland Legacy, A Family Saga Trilogy - western contemporary fiction
Book 1 – Lost In Wyoming – Lance's story
Book 2 – Moon Over Laramie – Tristan's story
Book 3 – Christmas In Cheyenne – Raul's story

Wyoming Christmas Trilogy – western contemporary fiction
Book 1 – Footprints In The Snow – Tom's story
Book 2 – A Visitor For Christmas – Brianna's story
Book 3 – Trapped On The Mountain – Chris' story

Summer Days In Wyoming Trilogy - western contemporary fiction
Book 1 – A Ride In The Afternoon
Book 2 – Fire At Midnight
Book 3 – Misty Meadows At Dawn

Old West Wyoming - western historical fiction
Book 1 - A Western Christmas
Book 2 - The Train To Laramie
Book 3 - The Last Stage Coach

Seattle Rain series - women's fiction novels
Book 1 - A Walk In The Rain
Book 2 – Rain, Again!
Book 3 – After The Rain

Virginia Lovers Trilogy - contemporary romance:
Book 1 – Alexandra's Garden
Book 2 – Ariel's Summer Vacation
Book 3 – Lulu's Christmas Wish

A Guest At The Ranch – western contemporary romance

Storm In A Glass Of Water – a small town story

CHAPTER 1

Laramie, Wyoming Territory, December 1887

Elliott Maitland was in a bad mood. It was so cold that he could hear the stones cracking. He would have liked a few more days of warmer weather, just so he could move his cattle from the exposed northern pasture closer to his ranch where he could watch over them better. Now he had to buy extra hay to see them through the bad weather.

He stopped his wagon in front of the old mercantile. The town was growing and there was a fancy store now, called Trabing Commercial Company store at the corner of Garfield and South Second Street. But Elliott preferred to do his business at the old mercantile.

The dark grey clouds hang ominously low and a few snowflakes were falling from the sky, announcing a big blizzard. Elliott cursed mentally. The weather was unpredictable and he had to make haste and return to his ranch north of town before the ground was covered in

1

white snow, and the visibility so poor that a man could get lost on his way to the outhouse.

"Hey Sam," he greeted the old curmudgeon, owner of the store. "I need a few things before returning home. Here is what I need." Elliott took out of his pocket a wrinkled piece of paper where he'd written a short list before leaving home.

The owner was not very friendly, but Elliott was not talkative either. People tended to mind their own business and not ask questions in these parts. So he was surprised when Sam started to make conversation while stacking Elliott's supplies.

"Mighty cold weather we're having," Sam said, looking at him sideways.

Elliott nodded and carried some of his supplies to the wagon. When he came back, he found Sam hopping from one foot to the other.

"What? The ants got to you?" he asked Sam, impatient to be on his way.

Sam scratched his bold head and moved closer. "Maitland, we're in a pickle."

A WESTERN CHRISTMAS

Elliott had been in difficult situations so many times in his life that he couldn't remember when he had not been in a pickle. "Sam, spit it out faster or the blizzard will catch me on the road."

Sam bent forward over his counter and Elliott was struck by a strong whiff of tobacco that the owner of the mercantile chewed. "You know that Miss Dunlop, the schoolteacher, left us and moved back to St. Louis. Not that anyone will miss her prune face."

"No, I don't know. I don't have kids who go to school."

"Right. But you might have one day." Elliott had enough trouble dealing with what life dished out every day, and taking on more was unthinkable. "Here is your chance," the shopkeeper continued. "The new schoolteacher arrived on today's train. Unfortunately, there was no one at the depot to welcome her, or to tell her where to go. It's right before Christmas. Because of this weather, the ranchers went home, the three hotels are full, and the rest of the lodgings are... somewhat rowdy. So, she came here." Sam said in a low voice, almost whispering. He inclined his head toward a person sitting on a chair near the potbelly stove in the middle of the room. "I am closing the store for the day soon, and I can't give her lodgings even if I wanted to." Sam lived in a small room at the back of his store.

"How about the boarding house on Sheridan?"

"It's full of the girls hired by Tom Wilkes for his saloon. We can't mix the schoolteacher with them."

"She could go to Dr. Pendergast. He never refuses anyone in need," Elliott suggested, eager to be on his way.

"Dr. Pendergast is busy patching up the cowboys who shot each other last evening at the saloon. And the pastor has no room in his house what with his wife just having given birth to their seventh child."

"Seven?" Elliott couldn't imagine having to take care of so many children.

"Right. So I think you should take her," Sam concluded and nodded, happy to have found a solution.

"Take her where?" Elliott asked, thinking there was no way he could make a detour and arrive home before the blizzard made it impossible to find any road.

"Home with you. She has nowhere to go and she can't stay here."

Elliott looked at Sam with horror. "Are you mad? I'm a bachelor. The ranch hands who stay with me over winter are rough men. All bachelors. When the busybodies in town find out she spent several days at my ranch, they'll have us married in no time at all."

"Yes, well, this is your chance to get married, boy. It's not like many women are knocking on your door. This is Wyoming. The town has grown, but good women are still scarce." Sam tried his best to convince him.

"You said she's prune faced."

"Not her, the other one who went back to St. Louis. This one is… Well, at least she's younger," Sam ended lamely.

"No way," Elliott shouted and looked at the woman sitting near the stove. She sat poker straight, with her hands in her lap looking straight ahead. She had a severe profile with a longish nose, accented by the funny hat perched on her head and adorned with some silk flowers and… were those cherries? Her hair, an uncertain shade of mousy brown, was tied in a bun at her nape.

Feeling his eyes on her, she turned her head slowly to look at Elliott. Her eyes were golden-brown, the best part of her, if not for the hint of desperation he detected in them. Then he saw that her gloves had two big holes she tried to hide and her jacket was carefully darned in several places.

"I'll take her," he heard himself saying.

"Good." Sam beamed at him. "Her trunk is up front."

The trunk was near the front door and it looked big enough to carry everything that Sam had in his store. Elliott was a tall man with muscles honed during long hours of work on the range. He lifted up the trunk on his shoulder and grunted from the effort. He dropped it in the back of his wagon near his supplies.

"Wait!" The woman came after him. "Where are you taking me?" she asked, catching her lower lip between her teeth with worry. She was torn between the need to find a warm house to rest and the fear of the unknown, especially this large man, with long dark hair and beard.

He didn't bother to answer her question. He just muttered, "Lord, woman, what do you have in this huge trunk? Millstones?"

"Books," she answered, looking at her trunk, which now rested in his wagon, half leaning onto bales of hay and an assortment of burlap sacks with supplies. "Listen, maybe it's not such a good idea. I think I could find lodgings in town somewhere."

"Not so close to Christmas, you can't. Not unless you want to live with the girls hired by the saloonkeeper, but then your teaching career will be at an end. The righteous ladies would be outraged. Let's hope that they'll understand that you had nowhere else to go and came with me."

She was undecided. A gust of wind penetrated through her thin jacket.

Elliott rummaged under the seat of his wagon and found a thick woolen blanket that he wrapped around her. "Do you see the low hanging dark clouds? It means the blizzard will be upon us soon. The closer we are to home, the better our chances of survival. Now, can you climb up in the wagon by yourself or do you need a push?"

She wrapped herself tighter in the blanket, grateful for the warmth, and tried to climb up on the seat. Either her limbs were tired or she tried too hard to preserve her modesty and not show her ankles, because after three attempts, Elliott lost his patience and, grabbing her by the waist, he hoisted her up on the bench.

Hmm, she felt nice and her curves very womanly to his touch. Elliott shook his head. He must have been without a woman for too long if he liked this stick of a schoolmarm. He climbed up and they were off.

The horses felt the bad weather approaching and sped up their pace. Soon they left behind the last houses in Laramie and followed the road to Elliott's ranch.

"I'm Celestine Tillman. Nice to meet you," the woman said burrowing under the blanket, yet succeeding to sound prim.

"I'm Maitland," Elliott grumbled, trying to see some familiar landmarks ahead to lead him home. They traveled in silence for a while. It started to snow in earnest and the landscape was a sea of white. A crop of rocks were good guidance.

The all white ground in front of them was almost blinding. Elliott heard the snarl before he saw the danger. He grabbed the rifle that always rested at his feet. It was more reliable at a distance compared to his guns.

"Hold this," he told Celestine and handing her the reins, he pointed the rifle toward the crop of rocks. However, when the attack came, it was unexpected. The mountain lion tried to jump on the horse closest to him. Neighing, the horse shied away. Elliott pulled the trigger. The predator fell to one side wounded, but still had enough life in him to run away.

"I hit it, but I didn't kill it. Too bad. A wounded animal is more dangerous than a healthy one," Elliott said, placing the Winchester at his feet. He considered going after the cougar, but then discarded the idea. It was already late and their priority was to arrive home as soon as possible. Preferably before dark.

He took the reins from Celestine and saw that she was holding them with her left hand, and in her right hand, she had one of the little toy-guns preferred by the card players. What do you know, the schoolmarm had gumption.

"What did you want to do with that toy, Celestine? Hit the mountain lion on his head?" Elliott asked, barely refraining from laughing.

She handed him the reins and placed the small gun in her reticule. "I'll have you know that a Derringer can be deadly at close distance. And what other choice do we, women have to protect ourselves? We can't strap big guns at our waist like men do," she explained, her feathers ruffled.

"Do you know how to use a gun?" he asked seriously this time.

She hesitated a moment before answering. "Yes. My father showed me how. The year before he was shot dead by his partner."

It was 1887 and civilization had extended into the west, but there were still robbers, outlaws, and other rough people. A man had to be prepared to defend his property and his family. The human being had only a thin veneer of civilization after all.

"Was it here in the west?" Elliott asked.

"No, it was back east in Philadelphia. My father and his partner owned a bank together. My father had just discovered that his partner had stolen a lot of money and had falsified the accounting books. That afternoon, someone shot him dead. Nothing could be proven. The partner vanished and the bank had to close. Everything we owned was sold to cover the debt." She related everything so matter-of-factly, like it didn't affect her directly. Yet Elliott saw a slight trembling of her lips, frequent blinking to stave off tears, and her hands clenched in her lap.

"I'll give you a better gun. You'll need it."

They were advancing at a slower pace now. The snow on the ground was slippery and it was difficult for the horses to trot. However, they were plodding on, knowing the way home with an innate sense that only animals had.

Elliott prodded the horses on, and finally breathed easier when he could see lights in the distance.

CHAPTER 2

When the wagon stopped in front of a sturdy ranch house, Celestine was so cold and covered in frosted snow that she would have been happy to see the smallest shack to warm her bones a little.

There was also a large red barn and a smaller building, the bunkhouse.

"Did you build all these?" Celestine asked.

Elliott looked around. "I only rebuilt the barn because the old one had suffered some fire damage and you could see the sky through the roof. The rest was already here, built by the previous owner."

Four ranch hands came from the bunkhouse.

"Hey Boss, we were ready to go search for you," said a tall, blond man with a friendly smile, looking at Celestine with curiosity.

A shorter man came closer to look her up and down. He wore his cowboy hat rakishly tilted to one side and adorned with a leather band and a silver concho. "Boys, the Boss brought himself a woman."

"Mind your manners, Joe," Elliott admonished him, jumping down from the wagon. "This here is the new schoolteacher. She came with today's train and nobody was at the depot to welcome her. She had nowhere to go." He extended his arms to help her get down.

The blond man nodded. "That's because rancher Miller has forgotten all about it. He's on the school board, what with his large brood of children."

"Yeah, I bet he forgot everything else when tragedy struck him," Joe added.

Celestine let Elliott grab her by the waist and set her down near the wagon. Her feet felt like jelly – the parts that she could still feel; the rest was frozen. She had to grab his arm not to collapse right there, near the wagon wheel. About the rancher that had failed to meet her at the train depot, she was a compassionate soul and understood the tragedy of losing a dear one and the despair of being destitute.

"Oh, poor man," she exclaimed. "Someone in his family died."

Joe waved his hand. "No ma'am. Precious got sick."

"Precious is rancher Miller's prize bull," Elliott clarified. "An ornery, mean creature, that wanders in our pastures and creates havoc among my cattle. But Miller would be ruined if Precious dies. He took out a big loan, guaranteed by his ranch, to buy that bull."

"I see," Celestine said, although she didn't understand how a bull could be worth as much as a ranch.

Elliott clapped his hands, to get their attention and to warm them up. "Celestine, this here," he said pointing at the tall blond man, "…is my foreman, Frank. You already met, Joe, who talks the most. The other ones are the Pirate, who works now and again when he pleases and I pay him accordingly, and Four Fingers, who is the best cook of us, but not by much."

Celestine nodded. The Pirate was a tall thin man, with a dark hair and a thin moustache curled at the ends, which he was grooming carefully. Four Fingers was an Indian man with long hair, in braids, under a black hat ornate with a feather.

Frank unhitched the horses and took them into the barn and the others started unloading the wagon.

Elliott guided Celestine up the three steps onto the porch and then opened the door and ushered her inside.

The first instinct was to cry, first of joy at the warmth inside the house, then of pain when her feet started to thaw. She looked with curiosity at the large kitchen where the stove was providing a lot of heat. Since the first catalogues were printed in the 1872 by Montgomery Ward and earlier this year 1887 by Sears, even the most isolated farms and ranches could order the newest appliances. This one looked rather new.

Then Celestine looked at the long table and she was dismayed. Unwashed tin plates and utensils, pans, and glasses filled the table. There was no table cloth and no napkins.

"We are a household of bachelors, Celestine," Elliott said, somewhat defensive, too proud to apologize. "And we didn't expect any guests. My first priority is the ranch and the cattle. Washing dishes comes last, if it comes at all."

The door opened again and Joe and Frank carried in her trunk. "Where do you want this, Boss?"

"In the parlor," Elliott answered inclining his head to the right. "The original homestead in 1878 only had this kitchen-living area and an alcove for the bed. Seven years ago, the owner added two more bedrooms, an elegant parlor, and improved the construction in general. However, the parlor is not used much. When a neighbor comes, we talk business, and ranchers prefer a cup of coffee and the comfort of kitchen to the stiffness of the fancy chairs. I got in the habit of using it for storage."

Celestine went to peek inside. A charming Victorian settee, upholstered in dusky rose velvet, with two matching chairs and a rosewood table with curbed legs were gathering dust in a room where no housekeeper had stepped in for several years. Her trunk was deposited in a corner of the room. Joe pushed the velvet brocade curtains and dust came out of them. How sad, Celestine reflected returning to the warmth of the kitchen.

Joe went to the door, then changed his mind and turned to her. He took his hat off hastily. He glanced at Celestine shyly, twisting his hat in his hands. "Ma'am, we thought... to ask you if you know how to cook. It's been a long time since we had a home cooked meal."

Frank stopped near him. "If Four Fingers hears you, you'll be in trouble."

"What? His biscuits are always burned on the outside and raw inside," Joe argued, still twisting his hat.

Elliott intervened. "Boys, I didn't bring Miss Tillman here to be our cook."

"Then why did you?"

"Because she had nowhere else to go. Let's not forget that she has traveled all day and she might be tired. Eastern ladies are delicate."

Celestine laughed. She had a very pleasant laughter. Not the giggling, tittering of other women. "Of course, I can cook something for supper if you show me where the supplies are. I can make very good biscuits. But it will take me another hour or more to clean this kitchen."

Joe moaned. "I'll clean the kitchen, while you get started on those biscuits."

How strange, Celestine thought later on, while mixing the dough for biscuits. She'd been frozen and tired, ready to lean her head on her arms on a table somewhere and sleep. Now she was warm and cooking. Too bad she was dressed in her best clothes to impress the school board president who had not bothered to come to the train depot to meet her because his bull was sick.

Ah, it couldn't be helped. Life was unpredictable. She should know. One day she was a carefree young woman engaged to the most desirable bachelor in all of Philadelphia. The next day, she had nothing. Not even a house to call her own. All had been lost. If rancher Miller had not offered her a position, she'd be in the poorhouse.

Celestine rolled up her sleeves and started to cook supper. It was too late to make a stew, which needed hours to soften the meat. Instead, she found salted pork, cut several generous slices, and fried them in the only clean pan she saw on a shelf. Then she peeled and sliced potatoes and withered carrots that she'd found in the cellar. She added a chopped onion and fried them all in the fat left from the pork.

She looked in the oven. The biscuits were golden and beautifully fluffed. She took them out and placed them in a basket covered with a cloth to stay warm. There was no churned butter for them, but in the cellar she found a small jar with honey.

She found a table cloth in a cupboard and set the table. When she finished and raised her eyes, she saw five pairs of eyes watching her with utmost attention. She extended her hand toward the table and they took their seats around the table still watching her.

Celestine considered herself lucky that, unlike her friends who wouldn't be caught dead cooking meals, she adored their family cook and had spent most of her time with her. She knew that five working men needed a lot of sustenance at the end of the day.

"Mr. Maitland, will you say grace."

Startled looks let her know that this was another

habit neglected in this household. But nobody protested. After Elliott grumbled a few words of thanks, they were ready to eat. The meat and potatoes disappeared quickly. Every now and then, a moan of pleasure was heard when they tasted her biscuits.

"Ma'am, this is the best meal I've ever had in my life," Joe declared, pushing his empty plate aside and sipping his coffee.

Celestine had learned that cowboys drank coffee at any hours of the day or night. Her suggestion that they should have tea in the evening was received with disbelief. She was a practical soul, so she let that go.

"Mr. Maitland, there are only a few days left before Christmas and I don't see any tree or ornaments here. Why is that?" Celestine asked.

A surprised look was the answer to her question. "We are working men, ma'am. We don't have time for embellishments."

Frank nodded in agreement. "It's a good thing we remember to wash our shirts. And then, it's either we take it in town to the washerwoman or we pull straws to see who got the short one to do the laundry."

Celestine sighed. They needed a woman. That was not going to be her. After the New Year, she would start teaching school in town. But she was stuck here until then. And she had promised herself that she would celebrate Christmas wherever she'd end up. Poor as she expected it to be, she'd find a scrawny, small tree to decorate with what ornaments she had. Christmas was special. It deserved to be celebrated.

"You know, my apple pie was famous in four counties and awarded prizes at the fair. Too bad we can't have a tree to decorate and to celebrate Christmas properly," Celestine said primly, looking down at her hands."

"An apple pie, real, homemade…," Joe said dreamily. "I'll bring you a tree. I saw a pine tree near the church."

"No, you should not cut down the trees in town." Celestine objected. It was true there were not many trees around here.

"I'll bring the tree," Four Fingers said, licking a

A WESTERN CHRISTMAS

few drops of honey from his… four fingers.

CHAPTER 3

Next morning at breakfast, Elliott was toying with the last bite of the perfectly done flapjacks on his plate. "How come you know to cook so well, Celestine? I thought rich girls don't enter the kitchen."

Celestine, with a starched white blouse, a little worn at the wrists from too much washing, was sitting on her chair, perfectly straight, her back not touching the back of the chair, and delicately sipping her tea. "My mother passed away when I was a little girl. She got influenza, started coughing, and she was gone in three days." Her voice quivered a little, betraying her emotion. "My father never remarried. From then on, it was just him and me. But I guess I needed a mother figure and I used to sit for hours in the kitchen, watching our cook, who was a very good woman. She taught me how to cook. I will always be grateful to her."

It was early, but the snowfall had stopped momentarily and Elliott intended to reach his cattle, before it would start snowing again later, as the dark clouds predicted.

The door opened letting in a wave of frigid air and a very agitated Joe. "Boss, the old battleaxe is on the warpath again. The weather cleared only a little and here she is coming to meddle in other folk's business."

"What battleaxe?" Celestine wanted to know.

Elliott sipped the last of his coffee and rose to go. "That's Miller's wife. The most meddlesome busybody in the whole county. She is the self proclaimed arbiter of proper behavior. I wonder how she found out you are here."

"This is a small town, Boss. Someone saw you leaving town and carried the word," Joe answered. "Me and the boys, we're going with the hay wagon to the northern pasture. Four Fingers said it will snow again tonight for sure. And he's never wrong."

Elliott nodded. "Go. I'll catch up with you after I get a rid of Mrs. Miller."

Joe pulled his coat tighter against the cold and went outside. The ranch hands were waiting in front of the barn, their horses saddled. But they didn't get to ride away. The wagon, driven expertly at high speed by a short woman, stopped in front of the homestead. Elliott came out on the porch with Celestine peeking out from behind his back.

"Elliott Maitland!" shouted the woman from atop her wagon seat, in a surprisingly strong voice for someone so short.

It was a promising show and a dress down to the strong man that was their boss, so the men didn't ride away. They stopped to watch the scene.

"I'm right here, ma'am. No need to shout," Elliott said calmly, crossing his arms over his chest and leaning against the porch post.

Celestine examined the newcomer. She was quite round, with a quivering chin and a moustache that could make the Pirate envious.

"Mr. Maitland, I heard that you absconded with the new schoolteacher yesterday. How could you, I ask? It is a heinous act, indeed," she proclaimed with righteous indignation.

"What's 'a...sconded?" Joe asked in low voice.

"It means, 'he ran away'," Frank explained.

"Sure he ran away. The blizzard was coming," Joe commented back, louder.

Mrs. Miller speared him with her eyes, then continued, "Well what do you have to say?"

Elliott shrugged. "She had nowhere to go. I did my Christian duty and offered her shelter."

This seemed to enrage the woman even more. "You and your men are all bachelors and you brought here a gently reared maiden?"

"Are you telling me I should have left her to sleep in the street, her being gently reared and such?" Elliott narrowed his eyes.

The woman shook her finger at him. "Don't you sass me, Elliott Maitland. I want to know if you are going to do your duty and marry the woman you compromised?"

"No," Celestine's voice sounded clearly as she stepped out from behind Elliott. Mrs. Miller's jaw dropped. Nobody had said to her such a final 'no' before. "When no one waited for me at the train depot as promised, Mr. Maitland acted as a gentleman. He offered me a place to sleep when I had nowhere else to go."

"Are you telling me you don't want him? I know he's not much to look at, but he is a rancher and has his own land," Mrs. Miller argued.

"I have no objections to him as a person. But when I will get married, or when he will, it will be because we choose to do so, not as an arbitrary imposition."

"But... but...," the woman sputtered. "...you don't understand. You have been compromised by living here with him. Nobody will accept you as a schoolteacher now."

"Oh yes, they will. You are going to turn right back and tell everyone in town that I slept in the house while Mr. Maitland spent the night in the bunkhouse with the rest of the cowboys and that is the truth. Otherwise I'll go straight to the judge and complain officially that your husband placed my life in danger and didn't come to meet me at the train as promised because he valued his stupid bull more than the life of a... gently reared maiden who had come to town to be a schoolteacher."

The woman opened her mouth, then snapped it shut. Finally, she recovered her voice and aplomb. "You should have gone to a hotel."

"The hotels were all full and the boardinghouse's rooms had been rented to the girls hired at one of the saloons. Do you think their company would have been more acceptable for the future schoolmarm?" Celestine asked, her voice apparently calm, but a slight tremor betrayed that she was very upset. Elliott placed his hand on her back to encourage her.

"The judge will understand how important the bull is to Emory?" Mrs. Miller continued to argue, albeit slightly hesitant.

"Will he? By then, the whole town will find out how I was treated by your family. Even the pastor and the good people in church. Without the teaching job, I have nothing left and nothing to lose."

Mrs. Miller's face contracted in anger. "We'll see what Mr. Miller will say about this." And she turned the wagon around.

"Yes, please do. And inform him that I have the letter with his promise to meet me at the train depot," Celestine said, looking at the departing wagon, wincing when with a sharp crack Mrs. Miller whipped the horses into a more rapid pace.

Joe whistled. "Wow! I never heard of anyone getting the best of Mrs. Miller." The other ranch hands made similar approving sounds, but Celestine was unsettled. She'd won the battle, but she'd made a powerful enemy. Her life would not be easy regardless of the outcome. Mrs. Miller would see to it.

"Another driver is on his way here," Elliott commented near her ear. "This is the most social life that we've had in a long time." Then he addressed the men. "You go and spread the hay before the snowfall and the night catch you standing here." When the wagon came closer, he breathed easier. "It's Prudence Parker, my friend John's wife. The Parker ranch is bordering mine to the east. I leave you in good hands Celestine. I have to go to check on my cattle. In case of danger, use the Winchester above the mantel." He mounted his own horse and rode after his men.

The woman who stopped her wagon in front of the ranch house and jumped down was average looking, with a big smile on her face. "Hello, I'm Prudence Parker. I'm glad we'll be neighbors." She clapped her hands in delight.

"I'm Celestine Tillman. Glad to meet a friendly face in this corner of the world. Please come in." Celestine led the cheerful woman inside and placed the teakettle on the stove.

Meanwhile Prudence continued to talk, while taking off her heavy jacket. "I crossed paths with Mrs. Miller. She was mad as a wet hen. I heard the entire story from our man Cody, who was in town this morning and talked to the depot master. So, are you going to marry Elliott Maitland?" she asked with an impish smile.

"No, I'm not. This is no reason for marriage."

"No wonder Mrs. Miller was so mad." Her new friend searched Celestine's face. She was serious this time. "Leaving the old biddy aside, life here is not easy for a woman alone."

"Life is not easy in the east either."

"Yes, but here we are barely civilized. This land was homesteaded ten or twenty years ago. Men here are rougher and tougher. They had to be in order to survive. It is better for a woman to have a good, hard-working man at her side. Elliott Maitland is all that and more. He came here only five years ago and bought this land. I don't know the details, but he's a strong man. You could do worse. I don't want to convince you. I'm not Mrs. Miller."

Celestine touched her hand. "I know. And I appreciate your advice, but… It's not right for either of us to marry under pressure. I just went through a nightmarish situation and my engagement was broken after my father died. I can't think of marriage. Elliott was kind to give me a place to sleep. I don't want to see him forced to marry me. He should be able to have the bride of his choice. Not a destitute, long-faced schoolteacher."

"Now, don't put yourself down, Celestine. You are a refined lady from the east, and women here are few and far between. Men don't have many choices. Trust me, life is hard and nights are lonely for a rancher if he has no wife."

Celestine set her cup down. "You are probably right. You know more about life here than I do. But I've had my share of misfortune and pain back east. I learned the importance of having a backbone. I'm not going to let anyone force me to do anything."

"How long are you going to live here with Maitland?" Prudence asked her, changing the subject.

"I'm not sure. For all her righteousness, Mrs. Miller didn't suggest a different alternative. Probably until after the New Year when classes begin."

"Good. The schoolteacher's house is nothing more than a shack, with a smoking fireplace that doesn't provide much heat and a far away outhouse. The shack is in a rather isolate place on the outskirts of town, and it's scary at night. Unsavory characters still plague the west."

"Until I move there, I intend to make myself useful, cooking good meals for the men."

"You're worth your weight in gold if you know how to cook. Men will flock to your door." Prudence rose, shook her skirts, and smiled at Celestine. "I have to go now. I'm glad to have a woman friend nearby. Life at the ranch tends to be rather isolate, no matter how busy we are."

CHAPTER 4

Elliott caught up with his men soon. His horse was a fast, half wild mustang, that obeyed only Elliott and sometimes not even him. He bought it five years ago, when he stopped in Laramie on his way to the west coast. He was at the train depot inquiring about a room for the night, when he saw a man whipping savagely a horse hobbled near a post. The horse had foam at his mouth and his skin was broken and bleeding.

Elliott didn't think. He just grabbed the other man's whip and broke it over his knee, despite the man's loud protests. When he saw him reaching for his gun, Elliott twisted his arm behind his back.

"You don't want to fight me. I'm faster and you'll be dead," he told the other in a lethal voice.

Having just gotten off the train that had carried him from as far away as Virginia, Elliott knew he looked like a naïve easterner, which he was, but a strong will and accuracy with a gun made him a credible opponent to all tempted to fool him.

"You can't do that. This is my horse and he's half wild. A stubborn vicious animal, that's what he is. He needs to be taught who the master is." The man looked again at Elliott. Then turned around, where the onlookers seemed to agree with Elliott and to express pity for the horse. "Tell you what. If you know better, why don't you buy my horse? I'll give it to you cheap and I'll throw in the saddle," he said shrewdly.

Elliott didn't think for too long what he was going to do with a horse on the train to San Francisco. He offered half what the other had asked and the deal was done. Coming from Virginia, Elliott knew a quality horse when he saw one and he'd gotten this splendid spirited animal very cheaply. The other man had pocketed some money and that was better than having to fight a good-for-nothing wild beast. In fact, he considered himself lucky that the easterner had come right when he thought he'd have to kill the worthless horse. He saluted and went to the saloon to enjoy his earnings from the deal.

It took Elliott more than an hour to coax the frightened animal to accept his touch. Then he took the horse by the lead to the stable and asked the man in charge to help him clean the horse's wounds. Then he fed him and left him there.

Tired, he went to the hotel and asked for dinner and a room for a night. That evening, his plans and his life changed entirely when he became the owner of the deed to a prosperous ranch north of town. He never intended to be a rancher, but life was indeed unexpected with surprising turns.

Next morning, after recording the land in his name at the land recording office in town, Elliott went to take his horse from the stable. The horse looked at him cautiously, sniffed his hand and let him place the saddle on. At the stable master's advice he bought a new, better saddle and rode away to his newly acquired ranch.

"What do you say, Red? We've been together ever since," Elliott said, patting his bay stallion. The horse nickered in answer.

He found his men near the hay wagon, looking at some tracks in the snow. There were only two, Frank and

Joe. "Where are the others?"

"Four Fingers went that way, toward the wilderness far north," Frank answered pointing there. "You know he doesn't talk much or explain himself. He just rides away to meditate or whatever he's doing communing with nature."

"He's communing in the snow? When it's so cold, even going to the outhouse is too much communing with nature." Joe commented.

"At least he told us not to expect him tonight."

"And the Pirate?" Elliott asked sighing. He had a bunch of unreliable men, who forgot who paid them.

"The Pirate just waved his hand and said he's going to town to find out what's new."

"More likely to drink and gamble," Elliott muttered.

"That too," Frank agreed. "But you must admit he is a great source of news about what happens in town. We are a bit isolated here, and the Pirate supplies the latest going-ons."

"That's not why I pay him."

"True. And you don't pay him much. It's a wonder where he gets his money," Frank said.

"He's a great gambler. He can win a hundred dollars in one night," Joe explained.

Frank whistled. "That much? My best win was two dollars. I had a good dinner and a fancy room at the hotel with it."

Elliott's attention was attracted by the tracks on the ground. There were footprints, animal prints, and farther was an arrow embedded in the snowy ground. He picked it up, then threw it away.

"What do you say, Boss? Were them Indians sneaking around?" Joe asked.

"What are you talking about?" Frank scoffed. "This is 1887. There haven't been any Indians roaming free on these lands for more than ten-fifteen years. Besides, look at Four Fingers. He has a good rifle and I doubt he knows how to use a bow with arrows. You read too many dime novels, Joe."

"It's true," Elliott agreed. "That arrow is a new artifact, like the ones used by Buffalo Bill in his shows.

It's not real."

They rode on and just when Elliott wondered if the three of them could drive the cattle closer to home, they found the largest part of them huddled together in a gully between two large rock formations.

"Look, I think they found a natural shelter from the weather. Let's unload the hay wagon and with feed they should be fine until the frosty weather goes away," Frank said.

"It's too close to Dargill Creek for comfort," Joe protested.

Dargill Creek was a spooky place, haunted by the souls of people who died mysteriously there, Indians and outlaws, and cowboys who had the guts to go there and then vanished. Cowboys were superstitious and believed these old legends. Not many people dared to go there now. It was a remote place, on the border between the Maitland and Parker ranches.

"Nonsense," Elliott said, spreading hay for the cattle. "There are no ghosts or haunted places. There are only bad people hiding there. We'll have to investigate."

Two identical horrified looks from his men were his answer. "But not now," he added to the relief of his men.

After Prudence left, Celestine tied at her waist the apron she'd found on a peg. She cut chunks of beef, and placed them in a large pot to cook for the stew. Then she went into the cellar to investigate the supplies. She didn't find dried apples for a pie, but she found canned peaches. Good for a cobbler. There were plenty of potatoes, beans, onions, and some withered carrots, and to her delight dried herbs packed in paper. She smelled thyme and sage. They looked old, but were not molded and she was sure she could coax some flavor out of them once in boiling liquid. No cinnamon or vanilla. But enough flour, sugar, and coffee. No tea.

Satisfied with what she'd found, she returned to the kitchen and, humming softly, she peeled the potatoes, diced them, and threw them into the pot.

She felt a strange sense of contentment that had been absent ever since her father had died. She always associated it with the warmth and flavors of the kitchen, but it was more than that. She felt safe for the first time since that fatal night when she'd found her father dead on the floor and his associate searching in her father's desk drawers, through the papers there.

She felt safer here in the Wild West, on a ranch in the middle of nowhere, living with rough cowboys. Safer than among the civilized Philadelphia society, whose members had turned their backs on her from the moment tragedy befell her. Close friends, her fiancé who had sworn eternal love, people her father had helped personally; they all pretended not to know her anymore after his death. She'd been destitute and abandoned by all.

Here, Elliott had given her shelter. She knew that he'd help her if she lost her teaching position. He would never turn his back on her if she was in need. Also Prudence, whom she'd just met today, seemed to be a more reliable friend than her girlfriends back east, known to her since childhood. She remembered how they envied her for having Richard as her fiancé, the most eligible bachelor in town. They whispered behind her back all the time that she was no beauty and he was more attracted to her father's money than to her.

They were right, and so was Papa, who'd warned her that Richard was a gambler and not good enough for her, but she'd been starry eyed and so much in love. She'd told her father that Richard was the one for her, her soulmate. And her father reluctantly agreed to her wishes. How wrong she had been! Richard had discarded her without even bothering to talk to her. He sent his man to collect the engagement ring, just when the sheriff was taking possession of her house and all the contents inside to compensate for the losses at the bank.

Celestine wiped a tear from the corner of her eye. No more. She'd survived and was ready to make a new life here.

She measured the flour for the biscuits and mentally made a list of what she needed for a more festive Christmas meal. Not much. Just some cinnamon and vanilla sticks and perhaps raisins and cocoa powder. She hoped Elliott would approve. From what she'd seen, he didn't seem to be rich, but he wasn't a pauper either.

She had churned butter from the fresh milk Joe had brought in this morning and they had three chickens that laid eggs regularly. The cowboys were partial to fried eggs in the morning, or they didn't know what else to cook.

She was caught up in thought and didn't hear the approach of a rider. Heavy steps sounded on the porch and the door was pushed open forcefully. Darn, she'd forgotten to latch it up as Elliott had told her before leaving. Trying not to betray her anxiety, Celestine turned to face the newcomer. He was tall, burly, middle aged, and had narrow, mean eyes.

"Don't you know how to knock on the door when you come to visit?" she asked, raising her chin.

"Ah, you're a hoity-toity one, as I heard people saying in town."

"If you mean that I have good manners, then yes, I do."

"I'm Crawford," he announced, like he were the king of England.

Celestine inclined her head. "Very well. I'm

Celestine Tillman, Miss Tillman to you." She wondered if she should add 'Nice to meet you', as politeness required, but decided against it. There was nothing nice in bursting through the door of other people's house, unannounced and unwanted.

"Ha!" he shouted, leaning his head backwards and looking at her. "You're not much to look at, certainly not a beauty. I heard in town how Maitland was faster than the rest of us bachelors, and ran away with the newly hired schoolteacher." Celestine was thinking how to answer to this insulting comment when he continued, "I thought you were a raving beauty. Instead, you are like the old one who left us, albeit younger. But the same long face and high in the instep."

"If you are finished producing insults, you can leave. Don't forget to close the door behind you," Celestine said, with as much dignity as she could muster.

"Nothing can faze you. I know your kind." He came closer. "Let's see if you're all ice or if you have some spirit in you." He came closer and grabbed her waist, only to feel something poking in his stomach. He looked down and saw a small gun in her unwavering hand. "You think you can keep me at bay with that toy?" he asked incredulous.

"The Derringer can be deadly, especially at such close range." His hand inched closer to the gun. "Hands up."

"You don't have the gumption to shoot me," he said, nevertheless raising his hands and looking at the small gun touching his shirt.

"You think not? I've seen my father shot dead by his associate and I've known the cruelty of so-called friends who didn't lend a hand when I lost everything, including the house where I was born. And I survived. Just try me. A single woman alone, attacked by a stranger. You'll be dead and no one will blame me"

He eyed her warily and then stepped back. "Oh, who needs you? Maitland can keep you." He raised his finger at her. "Tell him my patience is running thin. He should take my most generous offer and go, if he knows what's good for him. Nobody will pay more for this land."

"I doubt Mr. Maitland intends to sell his ranch, to you or anyone else," Celestine answered, primly still pointing her gun at him. She knew no such thing, but it was a good assumption. Besides, looking at this Crawford, she doubted his offer was anywhere near generous.

"He didn't homestead the land like the rest of us. He got it from a cards gamester. He should take whatever profit he can get and leave. Or his cattle will drop sick like Miller's prize bull." Saying this, Crawford made his exit, pulling the door shut after him with enough force to rattle the windows.

CHAPTER 5

Her knees shaking, Celestine collapsed in the nearest chair. She hoped Maitland was not going to give up his ranch because of those threats. And if he were to sell it in the end, she hoped it wouldn't be to a bully like Crawford. Maitland had a powerful enemy.

What about winning the ranch in a game of cards? Was it true? All men played cards. It was not unusual. But she was disappointed. Her ex-fiancé was a gambler, and she didn't approve of playing cards, especially for such high stakes like a ranch.

Sighing, Celestine checked on the stew and placed the large pan with biscuits in the oven. Then she started on the peach cobbler.

When the men returned later in the afternoon, the kitchen was warm and smelled of cooked meat, vegetables, and biscuits. They sniffed the air appreciatively and gladly accepted warm mugs with freshly brewed coffee.

The dinner was a success and the cobbler a

pleasant surprise. After they finished eating, Celestine told them about the visit she'd had from Crawford.

"Yeah, I know. Crawford is as ornery as Miller's bull. He is pressuring me to sell him my land. In his dreams," Elliott said with conviction.

"He implied that your cattle will drop sick just like Miller's bull," Celestine remembered. "Does this mean that he poisoned the bull and threatened to do the same with your cattle?"

"I wouldn't put it past him, ma'am," Frank answered her.

Celestine looked at Elliott sideways. "He said that they all homesteaded here, while you won the ranch in a game of cards, and you shouldn't be attached to the land."

Elliott looked at the last of his coffee and set the mug on the table. "It's true I was not the first one who settled here. The first one was an outlaw turned sheriff in the 1860s, when Laramie was just founded. He died unexpectedly. His son, a youngster of eighteen, took to gambling. He was no match for a professional gambler, who had a few tricks up his sleeve. I don't know if he cheated or not, but the youngster lost the ranch. I was traveling on my way to San Francisco when I stopped in Laramie for a night. I was at the hotel when I heard the card player complain that winning a ranch was not his goal and he would sell it cheaply to the first one to offer him cash."

Joe slapped his knee. "Really? I always wondered how you got to be a rancher."

"I didn't intend to. Not even then. I thought it was a good opportunity. If the deed was valid, then the price was not bad. We bargained and went to the Land Recording agent who confirmed that it was legit. So I bought it and registered it in my name. It was all legal. Next day, the young man came to complain. The gambler was long gone from town, but the judge confirmed that whatever had happened the day before, I was now the legal owner of the ranch, house, furniture, and all. I offered to house the young man until he found another situation, but he left town in a huff."

"Then what did you do?" Frank asked.

"I still planned to sell the ranch. What did I know about raising cattle? After the owner had died, the ranch hands had left one after the other, so I had more or less an abandoned ranch on my hands. I intended to leave it myself when Four Fingers knocked on my door. He told me to hire two more men and round up the cattle that were scattered all over the land. The struggle to make this ranch work and profitable was hard, but I am an ambitious man. I couldn't quit before succeeding. And when I did, and the ranch showed a profit, I realized that this was home now. Where would I go?"

Celestine touched his hand and brought him back from the memories of the past. "Mr. Maitland…"

"Call me Elliott."

"I couldn't. What would people say?"

"They already do. They say a lot, most of it false, and you can't change their narrow minds. We live here, call me Elliott."

"Very well, Elliott. Interesting story. I'm glad you are not a gambler."

Elliott rose and pushed his chair back. "Good

meal. Thank you, Celestine."

"I'm sorry the other two men didn't get to enjoy it."

"Yes, they leave from time to time for parts unknown."

Celestine looked at him shyly. "I made a short list, a few things I need to buy for our Christmas dinner. It's not much, some cinnamon and vanilla, cocoa... I found a lot of supplies in the cellar, but not dried apples. I would like to go to town tomorrow." She was wringing her hands, not knowing how to explain that she had no money at all and who knew when Mr. Miller would pay her or if he still intended to give her the position.

"Go to the mercantile and buy everything you need. Tell Sam to put it on my tab. And Celestine, don't scrimp on anything. I discovered that after five years, I'm hankering after a nice celebration with good food. Joe will drive you to town."

Next morning, Celestine was frying eggs and bacon, when she heard loud voices outside. She transferred the eggs from the pan to a large platter and went outside to see what the ruckus was about.

Four Fingers was untying a nice size pine tree from the travois at the back of his horse. Joe and Frank were assisting him, peppering him with questions about where he'd found it and where he'd been.

Celestine clapped her hands in wonder. Considering there were no trees at all around them, it was a miracle indeed. "Oh, you brought me a tree. Oh, dear man." The prim and controlled schoolteacher was jumping up and down with excitement, her golden-brown eyes lit with joy, like a little girl. She even kissed Four Fingers' cheek, and darn if the Indian didn't blush under his tanned skin.

Leaning against the barn door, Elliott watched mesmerized, how changed Celestine was. In this moment, she looked beautiful, all glowing with happiness. He was almost jealous of Four Fingers for being the one to put that glow on her face.

"Let's set it in the parlor, in a bucket with rocks and some water," Celestine suggested. "I cleaned the room the best I could and I dusted the curtains."

The men looked at one another disappointed.

"Why in the parlor? Nobody ever goes in there."

Celestine blinked. "That's how it has always been." The men had a good point. They practically lived in the large kitchen, all of them. The Christmas tree was set in the parlor for the visitors to see in Philadelphia's high society, but it didn't mean that they had to do the same here. "By all means, let's place it in the kitchen, in front of the window on the right. Far from the stove. I'll decorate it when I come back from town."

And so it was done. All the way to town, Celestine talked about her most beautiful tree, and how all she had hoped for before was a tiny tree in the corner of a drafty room somewhere. And now, look what a celebration she would have…

Joe dropped her off in front of the mercantile and promised to return in an hour. When she entered the store, two other ladies were coming out. Celestine smiled at them, but after a brief look up and down, the ladies looked straight ahead and left the store.

Celestine shrugged. Not everybody was as happy as she was to have such a beautiful tree. "Good morning, Mr. Sam."

"Just Sam," muttered the surly shopkeeper.

"Here is a list of supplies I need. Put it on Mr. Maitland's tab. That's what he said." Celestine looked around and, with the few meager pennies she had, she bought some licorice, a pair of gloves for Four Fingers, and a red scarf for Frank. She already had some gifts in her trunk for Joe and Elliott.

Sam placed it all in two burlap bags.

"Hold on to them until Joe comes to pick me up. I'll walk through town until then," Celestine let him know.

The shopkeeper coughed, looked around his empty store, and whispered in a conspiratorial tone, "Miss, I feel a bit responsible for you, 'cause you came to my store first and I foisted you on Maitland. But I had no idea what else to do."

"What are you talking about?" Celestine asked, not understanding what he was trying to say.

"It's like this. That meddlesome old biddy, Mrs. Miller, I'm sure it was her, spread the rumor in town that you are living in sin with Maitland. I know how you came to be with him, 'cause I suggested. But you continued to stay with him. I hope you know what you are doing, and that Maitland will marry you. He's an honorable man, and I don't know what else you can do."

Celestine smiled at him to reassure him. "I thank you for your concern, Mr. Sam. But as I told Mrs. Miller, nothing untoward took place and Mr. Maitland is sleeping in the bunkhouse with his men. I refuse to be coerced to marry."

"That's all great, but you'll be coerced, as you say, if they won't give you the schoolteacher's position. Life is hard here for everyone, especially for a woman alone," the shopkeeper said with understanding.

Celestine considered the situation seriously. She was stubborn, but she didn't want to ignore reality. She had a practical nature. "Tell me, Mr....Sam, are rooms available at the hotel?"

"Not this close to Christmas, no. I don't know

who is visiting us, but it's crowded in town. I even sold an expensive porcelain doll I've had for years."

"How about the boarding houses? Are there any free rooms?"

The shopkeeper scratched his head. "No, ma'am. The saloon next to the rail tracks brought in a troupe of actors to act and sing. They occupied all the rooms that the saloon girls didn't."

"There is your answer. Even if I wanted to move, and I don't, there would be nowhere to go. So, I'll just stay right where I am and celebrate Christmas with nice people." Celestine nodded and smiled at him. "I appreciate your thinking of my wellbeing. I'll be back." And she left the store.

The shopkeeper shook his head and looked after her. She was a nice lady, and the busybodies in town were set to chase her away with her reputation in tatters. It was such a pity. Maybe if he talked to the pastor…

CHAPTER 6

Celestine left the mercantile and walked slowly on the boardwalk. She stopped in front of a dressmaker's store to admire in the window an exquisite creation of a blue dress with three layers of lace bordering the skirt draped over an underskirt with stripes of the same blue. The top had a lace border. The whole elaborate ensemble was completed by a large bow of a lighter blue on top of the back bustle. This was really pretty. It must have taken a lot of hours of work for the seamstress to achieve such perfection.

The door opened and the same two ladies Celestine had met at the mercantile exited the store.

"...be ready in time," was the parting shot of the taller one who pulled the door shut after her with more force than necessary. Unfortunately, she was not done venting her anger. Looking at Celestine she said, "It's surprising that Mr. Miller hired a woman with low morals to teach our children. What is the world coming to?"

Celestine was stunned by such an attack. But she

quickly recovered her poise and dignity. "You don't know me at all. How can you judge me?"

"You live with all the uncouth men at the Maitland ranch, don't you?"

"The ranch hands and Mr. Maitland have better manners than you and they certainly know how to treat a lady, which apparently you don't."

The tall lady huffed and walked away, taking her haughty attitude into another shop. Her friend looked at Celestine with less hostility, but she shrugged and hastened to catch up with the tall woman.

"Darn, I shouldn't have lost my temper," Celestine muttered.

"I'm glad you did."

She heard a voice behind her. She turned and saw a young woman about the same age as Celestine, smiling at her warmly. That was a first in this town, where she'd seen no friendly face, except for Maitland and his men. She returned the smile. "Hi, I'm Celestine Tillman. Nice to meet you."

"I'm Emily Parker, proprietor of this shop. I'm

glad to know the person who got the best of Cora Lynn Turner, the self-proclaimed queen of this town. Her husband owns the bank and is thirty years older than her."

Celestine processed this information. It wasn't good news for her and her teaching career. "Then, I'm afraid I don't have a future in this town, after antagonizing such an influential person."

"Sure you do. Cora Lynn likes to criticize and feel superior, while Mrs. Miller is a busybody. The truth is that they've had trouble finding a teacher. Women are scarce in the west and lonely ranchers fight to marry them. The teachers either marry or return back east. Either way, the school board needs to search for another. They'll let you teach and say thank you, if they don't want another qualified teacher to leave."

That was reassuring. If indeed the board would not be convinced by Mrs. Miller that she was of low morals, Celestine thought. In the distance, the train whistled coming in the depot.

"Tell me, are you related to Prudence Parker?

She's such a nice person."

Emily hesitated before answering. "I was married briefly with Parker's cousin. He died. Parker is still mourning his death. I don't." Her eyes had that lost look of a person caught up in unhappy memories.

"Oh, I'm sorry," Celestine said, not knowing what else to say and not wanting to pry.

"Don't be. He was not worth it. He presented to the world a charming and carefree personality, but in reality he was an abusive, selfish man. He died in another woman's bed, shot by her husband. At the time, I was so fed up with him and his constant put downs, that I was ready to overlook cheating if only he'd leave me alone…." Emily shivered, both because of the cold and bad memories. "Come in to have tea and talk about happier things."

A tall man passed by and inclined his head in a silent greeting, but didn't stop to say hello or to talk. First, Celestine thought he was avoiding her due to the rumors, but then she saw her new friend blushing to the roots of her auburn hair. "Who is he?" she couldn't resist asking.

"That's Lloyd Richardson. He has a ranch in a remote area near a canyon, northwest of town. We were close a few years ago, but then he went to Denver and I married Fred Parker. We lost touch."

"And now he's back."

"Yes, he had to take over the family ranch after his older brother was gored by a bull. Let's go inside," Emily invited her.

She opened the door to let Celestine inside, when a young man came running. He halted to a stop in front of them. "Miss Tillman, Sam sent me after you. You had a telegram. It came yesterday. Here." He handed her a piece of paper.

Celestine opened it. "Looking for you. Good news. Letter following." It was signed Humphrey Dunn, Attorney-at-Law. Dunn had been her father's lawyer, who was very active after her father's death, but in the end, he couldn't prove anything or save her from destitution. She'd lost everything.

"Good news?" Emily asked and the young man

looked at Celestine interested to hear.

"So he said in the telegram. No details. But he's a layer and used to claim all sorts of things, true or not," Celestine answered, pocketing the telegram.

The young man departed, disappointed that he had no exciting news to impart to others about her.

He almost crossed paths with another man riding at high speed. He stopped in front of them, but didn't dismount. "Miss Tillman. Joe is fighting in front of the saloon. Three jumped on him. He told me to take care of you."

"Where is the saloon?" Celestine asked.

"Follow me," he answered, turning his horse and riding back. Celestine picked up her skirts and ran after him. She reached the saloon with her hat askew, a cherry dangling in front of her eyes.

Men and saloon girls were standing outside, looking at two burly men holding Joe by the arms, while the third one was hitting him as if he were a punch bag.

Celestine didn't think. "Stop," she cried. Raising her reticule where she carried one of her precious books, she hit him in the head. Stunned, the man turned to see what hit him. "Have you no shame, three of you against one? Are you cowards?" And for good measure, she raised her reticule and hit the other two, who were surprised and let Joe drop to the ground. She turned to face the first man, just in time to see him reaching for his gun. She stepped forward and in a second her Derringer was pressed to his chest. "Do it and you'll be dead."

He looked at her in disbelief. "Lady, do you intend to fight all three of us with that little toy gun."

"I don't have to. If my hand trembles only a little, you'll be dead. Make your cohorts understand that."

He looked at her still undecided, when a strong voice interfered, "That's enough. There will be no fight. You three, take your guns and horses and leave town."

Celestine turned to see a tall man with a dark Stetson, pulled low over his brow. She saw a shiny star on his shirt under his jacket. "You're the sheriff?"

He sketched a slight bow. "Bill Monroe, at your service, ma'am. Please put that toy... pistol away."

Celestine looked at the three men who mounted

their horses and rode away. Then at the onlookers, who were returning in the saloon, now that the fight was over. "Where were you when they started punching Joe? And why didn't you arrest them?"

"I was at the train depot investigating a theft. And if I were to arrest every man involved in a fight, my jail would burst at the seams. Here at the saloon, men play cards, drink… do other things. Spirits are high and there are fights everyday."

"Yes, but, look at Joe, he's been beaten by three men. That's not a fair fight," She argued, looking at Joe, bloody and coiled on the ground, moaning in pain.

The sheriff cracked a smile on his somber face. "Luckily he had you to even the odds, ma'am. Even if I were to arrest them, they'll argue to the judge that Joe cheated at cards, insulted one of them, or looked lewdly at the girl who was with them. They'll be free in no time at all," he explained patiently in the same even voice.

"Are you telling me there is no justice out here in the west?"

"Of course, there is," he protested offended. "We

hang horse thieves and shoot bank robbers on sight. We have bounty hunters who chase outlaws and we form posses to catch robbers or murderers."

"I'm glad to hear." Celestine was tired of arguing and Joe needed help. "Can you tell me where the doctor is?"

"The second street to the left. There is a big sign on the door. You can't miss it," one of the saloon girls, who lingered behind, answered her.

Just when Celestine was wondering how she was going to carry Joe to the doctor, the sheriff picked him up and threw him on his horse before climbing in the saddle behind him.

Well, if Joe didn't have his ribs cracked before, it was a good chance he had now – Celestine thought, following the sheriff to the doctor.

It was indeed a large house, with a sign announcing: Alfred Pendergast, MD.

The sheriff assured Celestine that they were lucky the good doctor was in town. Usually he was gone to one ranch or another when an emergency was called. Of course they had another doctor, but that one was usually drunk.

The doctor was a jovial little man, with a taller wife, quite sour-faced who acted as his nurse.

"What do we have here?" he asked rubbing his hands with soap and water. "The young man got into a fight?"

"Yeah, with the three men newly hired by Crawford," the sheriff answered.

"Crawford?" Celestine asked. "He visited Mr. Maitland's ranch and wanted to buy it. He was very threatening."

"Yeah, I heard he bullied Richardson too, but no luck. Richardson is a tough nut to crack," the sheriff commented. "Now, I have to go. There are three men in my jail and one is a wanted fellow." He saluted and left.

CHAPTER 7

"So, you are the famous Miss Tillman?" the doctor asked her, while cleaning a cut on Joe's brow.

"Famous?" Celestine croaked.

"We are a small town. News that the new schoolteacher left with Elliott Maitland spread like wildfire," he explained smiling, unfazed by Joe's moaning, working methodically to clean and bandage his cuts and bruises. "And now this, as the sheriff said, to even the odds and fight three men in front of the saloon."

"I had no choice. Look at Joe. I couldn't let them kill him. As for living at the Maitland ranch, it's not my fault that Mr. Miller didn't meet me at the train depot. There were no decent lodgings to be found in town," Celestine protested with indignation.

"A young woman should always behave with decorum and modesty," the doctor's wife added her two cents, twitching her long nose with distaste.

"Yes, my dear, you're right," the doctor said to his wife, before Celestine started to argue. Then he turned back to her. "We understand your circumstances, but the gossip was too interesting not to spread. No woman had stepped on Maitland's ranch since he took possession of it... We are not a bad town. Some of us are really likable. Just give us a chance."

"I'm afraid they are not giving me a chance. They judged me and condemned me without knowing me," Celestine answered sadly.

"Not so. We are a curious, gossipy bunch. But we are not stupid. We need a schoolteacher, and finding a qualified person willing to come here is difficult, especially in the middle of the school year."

The doctor's wife returned to the room. "The pastor is here."

"The pastor?" Celestine exclaimed. "Is Joe's condition so bad?"

The doctor laughed. "No, of course not. In a couple of days, he'll be as good as before. The pastor is a good friend of mine. And of everyone in town who needs him."

The pastor was an average looking man, with

kind eyes and an easy smile. "Miss Tillman, I'm glad to finally meet you. Are you going to come to our church?"

"Of course. Christmas is in a few days and I wouldn't miss the service," Celestine hastened to assure him.

"Good, good. I was planning my next sermon from Luke, 'Don't judge or you'll be judged'. And of course we have a nice Nativity scene and my wife surpassed herself with the decorations this year."

"I can hardly wait."

Celestine left Joe at the doctor and went to the stable where the wagon and the horses were. The stablemaster knew Joe well and he looked at her with respect for saving Joe from the three men.

Sam, however was another story. Celestine stopped the wagon in front of the mercantile, mentally thanking her father for teaching her useful things like driving a buggy and a team of horses. While other girls spent their time embroidering, her father encouraged her to read books and to widen her horizon.

Sam hovered near the door of his shop and ushered her inside closing the door. "Tell me Miss Tillman, how is it possible that the refined eastern lady, who entered my store only a few days ago, is now the talk of the town. I know the reasons why you went with Maitland because I suggested it. But today, instead of proving to the good people in town what a proper schoolteacher you will be, I heard you embroiled yourself in a fight in front of the saloon no less. You hit two men with your purse and threatened one with a gun you carried on your person."

"Three. There were three men. And they were beating Joe."

Sam looked up at the ceiling in exasperation. "Men do occasionally get into fights and Joe can hold his own."

"No, he couldn't. Not this time. Two were holding him and the third was punching him."

"Nevertheless, women don't get into a fracas. They cover their eyes or even faint to prove how delicate they are."

Celestine had had enough. "I'm not delicate. If I'd been, I'd be dead. You tell the gossipy people in town that given a chance I'll do it all over again. The three men were intent on killing Joe. They had been hired recently by Crawford. What rancher hires three new men in the dead of winter when there is not much work to be done? Those men didn't know the head from the tail end of a cow. I bet they never did a day of work on the range in their life."

The store was empty, but Sam looked around and bent over the counter. "You think Crawford hired them to…"

"I don't think, I know. He came the other day to the ranch and threatened Mr. Maitland that if he's not selling his ranch to Crawford his cattle will drop sick like Miller's bull." Sam looked at her horrified. "So, get down from your high horse, Sam. I will not step aside and pretend nothing is going on. Maitland and his men were nice to me and I'll help if I can."

Sam loaded the bags with her shopping and another larger one he said was necessary for Christmas and she drove back to the doctor's office.

The doctor and his wife wrapped Joe in a thick blanket and helped her lift him up in the wagon among the bags from the mercantile.

"Just follow the road north, Miss Tillman and at the taller crop of rocks, turn right onto the country road. You can't miss it. The first ranch is Miller's, then Maitland's and Parker's is last. There the road ends."

She thanked them profusely, wrapped herself in another blanket and climbed in the seat. With a last wave to the kind doctor, Celestine was on the way. She had the Winchester at her feet and the weather was not so frigid. Her gloves provided adequate protection against the cold.

The road north was covered with snow, but was quite clearly marked by wheel traces and horse prints. So far so good. Joe was not unconscious and if in need, he could point to the right direction.

After they left town, the field was rather deserted, and they rode in silence for a while. Such immensity, an ocean of white. For a person raised in the middle of a big and busy city, this was an impressive view.

"Be careful of the mountain lions," Joe muttered from under his blanket.

But it was not the mountain lions that disturbed the peace of the deserted landscape.

Celestine had just reached an outcrop of rocks and was wandering if she should turn right. But where? She turned to ask Joe, when she saw riders coming after them. They were four of them, and Celestine stopped the wagon. She had no chance of outrunning them. Better to face them straight on. She picked up the Winchester. She saw that without asking questions, Joe held out his hand with a Colt in it. But when the riders were almost upon them, he relaxed and withdrew his hand under the blanket.

The one in front, apparently the boss, rode closer to the wagon and looked at it and at Celestine. He touched his hat in salute. "Howdy, ma'am. I'm John Parker."

Celestine breathed easily. "Prudence's husband? I'm Celestine Tillman and I live temporarily at the Maitland ranch."

"I know. Prue told me." He smiled under his moustache. "Besides we are coming from town. We heard what happened to Joe." He looked in the wagon at Joe's battered face. "Hmm, I've been in my fair share of fights, what man hasn't? But you look rather bad, Joe."

"That was no ordinary fight, Mr. Parker. They were vicious. Newly hired by Crawford. He wants Mr. Maitland's ranch. The sheriff said Crawford wanted to buy Lloyd Richardson's ranch too."

Parker shook his head. "No way. Richardson would fight till the end. He'll never sell. Let us escort you to the ranch, ma'am. You'll be safer."

"Yes, thank you. I was wondering if I had to turn right and where."

They didn't travel long and the last rider from Parker's men shouted, "Riders coming from across."

"Stop the wagon," Parker commanded.

He and his men placed themselves between the wagon and the approaching riders.

"The fools are riding at high speed. On a field covered with snow, it can be treacherous. There are holes or rocks under the snow."

Indeed, one of the riders slowed down and was left behind by the other two who continued fast ahead. Seeing Parker and his men in front of the wagon gave them pause, but the leader waved his hand in dismissal.

"Parker, we know you. This is not your fight. Give us the woman. Boss wants her."

"You know my name, but you don't know me. My father settled here and survived by sticking together with our neighbors and helping each other. You are wrong. This is my fight. We defend our land and protect our women. Tell your boss that I am making it my fight." Parker cocked his gun and pointed at the rider. "Turn around, mister. This is not your land."

The second one made the mistake of pulling out his gun. It was shot right off immediately by Parker.

"Don't make the mistake of thinking a rancher is no match for a gunslinger. Yes, I heard at the train depot that Crawford had hired a big shot. It won't make any difference. Now leave."

"We'll be back," the rider threatened once more,

but turned his horse and rode away.

"Thank you, thank you, Mr. Parker. I don't know what I'd have done without you," Celestine told him, taking the reins.

"I'm sure you'd have thought of something, ma'am. I heard you are very resourceful," Parker joked. "In fact, I'm glad you let us deal with Crawford's men. For a moment, I was afraid you'd interfere and give them a piece of your mind."

CHAPTER 8

When Celestine stopped the wagon in front of the house, Elliott came running from the barn. "What happened? When I saw it was getting late and you had not returned, I was saddling my horse to ride to town."

He looked in the wagon and saw Joe, all swaddled up to his brow in a blanket. He opened his mouth to ask again what happened, when John Parker forestalled him. "Let's go inside Elliott and I'll tell you briefly the whole story. I can't stay long. Prudence will be worried if I don't get home before dark."

Elliott nodded to his friend to go inside, but first he grabbed Celestine by the waist and lifted her down from the tall wagon seat. Then he looked her up and down to assure himself she was all right and after that he followed Parker into the house.

Frank and the Pirate carried a moaning Joe to the bunkhouse. Four Fingers grabbed the burlap sacks from the mercantile.

"Well, look here. This sack is moving."

Celestine looked in the wagon to see what he was talking about. One of the burlap sacks was indeed moving and they heard a soft whining sound from inside.

"What did you buy that is moving, Miss Celestine?"

"Me? Nothing that was moving or whining I assure you."

From inside the sack, a tiny head with two round black eyes like two beads looked back at them.

"It's a puppy," Celestine exclaimed.

The little dog was shivering with cold and perhaps fear of unknown people. It was more than Celestine could resist. She extended her arms and picked him up. The dog nestled in her arms and stuck his nose under her chin and Celestine fell irrevocably in love with the small, helpless creature with soft, silky fur.

"Oh, he's so adorable," she said.

"He has a red bow at his neck with a scrap of paper," Four Fingers observed.

Celestine looked at it. "It says Merry Christmas. The sweet, dear man. He gave me a puppy for

Christmas."

Four Fingers looked at her surprised. "Who is this man, Miss Celestine?" Just when the ranch hands thought that a miracle had happened and their boss had found himself a nice woman who could cook, this unknown 'sweet man' was courting her and giving her gifts?

"Sam," she answered, still petting the little dog.

"Sam who?"

"Sam from the mercantile."

That left Four Fingers open-mouthed in surprise. The bald shopkeeper was a grumpy, cantankerous old man. Nobody in his right mind would call him sweet or dear. Not to mention that he was chewing tobacco all the time and it made him smell awful. Who could understand women? "I think Boss is a much better looking man," he muttered under his breath, carrying the other bags in the house.

"Of course Mr. Maitland is the handsomest man I know," Celestine agreed, hugging the puppy to her chest.

Inside the house, John Parker was ready to go after giving Maitland a short version of what had happened in town. "Unfortunately, we have to be prepared to fight. Crawford means to force us to sell. I don't know about Miller. If he loses his bull, he's not going to want to fight. His sons are not interested in ranching. Maybe we could buy him out," he concluded placing his hat on. But it was one more thing he wanted to say. "You've got yourself a feisty one in Miss Tillman. She's the right woman, able to face the hardships of life on the ranch. Be careful and don't squander the opportunity, my friend."

He opened the door and came face to face with Celestine. He stepped aside to let her in. "What do you have there, Miss Tillman?" he asked, scratching the puppy behind his ear.

"A Christmas gift from Sam," she answered.

Parker frowned. "Who's Sam?"

Four Fingers placed the burlap sacks in a corner of the kitchen. "That grouchy old man who keeps the mercantile."

"Ah, you see, you already have competition," Parker told Elliott, winked and left.

Later, after the ranch hands went to the bunk house and the dishes were done, Elliott lingered over a last cup of coffee.

"Cute fellow," he said looking at the puppy snoring happily, curled on Celestine's lap. "Did you have a dog when you were a child?"

"No, I didn't. I never thought about having one. I like dogs very much, but after Mama died, life changed entirely. I had responsibilities, including taking care of Papa. It was not a normal, carefree childhood. And Papa, it was like he felt something could happen to him too, and he wanted to teach me as much as possible to give me the best chance to survive without him. It's strange, but it never occurred to him to find me a husband to take care of me. Maybe he didn't know anyone he trusted."

"Did he give you the Derringer?"

"Yes, he did. And he taught me to shoot, to drive, and to think for myself." Celestine shook her head to chase the melancholy away, before the tears pooled her eyes and she made a cake of herself. "What about you?

Did you have a dog when you were a little boy?" She asked to change the subject. She realized that she didn't know much about him, except that he was an honorable man, hard-working, and helping the ones in need.

"Not really, no," he answered twirling absently the remains of his coffee in his cup. He was reluctant to talk, not so much because he didn't want to tell her, but because he didn't want to remember. Nightmares had to be kept at bay. "When I was eight I found a stray dog in the street. He followed me home. He was hungry I guess. We lived in Virginia and my father was an apothecary. We were neither rich nor poor. My father told me that I was a thoughtless little boy to bring a dirty animal in the house of an apothecary. Next day the dog vanished and I never saw him again."

"How sad! Couldn't you find another family to take him in?" Celestine asked, hugging the puppy to her as if afraid someone might take him away.

"No, I couldn't. Whoever got rid of the dog, probably my father or my elder brother, did it early in the morning. I searched down by the river, but there was no trace of the dog," he said sadly, giving her a hint that his family life hadn't been very happy.

Leave it alone – her good manners told her not to pry. Nevertheless she asked. "Why did you leave Virginia and your family, Elliott?" It was not only curiosity to know more about this man who had been so kind to her, but also the feeling that he had no one else to talk to. He hesitated, and she added, "There is drama in everyone's life. You don't have to tell me yours, if you don't want to."

"When I was in my teenage years, my father expanded his business and bought four other stores all over Northern Virginia. He became quite prosperous. My older brother was the heir of it all. In good English style, the eldest inherited all and the youngest had to make his own way in life."

"This is so unfair," Celestine protested.

"It's all right. I was told what to expect ever since I was a kid. My father ignored me most of the time, when he didn't find fault with what I had done and belittled me or taught me the right way with his belt. I went to work at a bank when I was twenty and by the time I was twenty-six, I had some money of my own and had been promoted several times. Being a bachelor, I was still living at home. There was no lost love between my father, who was a dour and severe man, my brother who was his carbon copy, and me. I was not a rebellious young man, but I was different."

"Nothing wrong with that."

Elliott was lost in his own memories. "It all blew up when my maternal grandfather died unexpectedly and left everything he had to me. It was not a fortune, but it was a respectable amount of money. You see, my father counted on that money to buy yet another store. In fact, he considered that he could use the money as he pleased and was surprised when the lawyer told him he needed my approval and when I flatly refused him. Let me be clear, he expected the money from me for free. Not as loan, not as investment in his business. I needed everything I had to make my own way in life without a penny from him. The next day, my place at the dining room table had been removed. My father informed me that an unnatural son, who doesn't help his father, is not welcome at his table or in his house."

Celestine covered her mouth with her hand. "Oh, how cruel of him. No son deserves to be treated this way..."

"So, I placed a few clothes and books in a suitcase, and I quit my job. I took all my money with me, and left on the first train going west. I intended to go to San Francisco and see what opportunities life offered there. As you know, I didn't get that far. I stopped in Laramie and you know the rest."

"Did you want to be a rancher?"

"Not in my wildest dreams. But Crawford is wrong. I bought this land on a whim, but I worked tirelessly to make it prosperous and it is my home now. This is my corner of the world, my place on earth where I'll live, work, and die."

The puppy whined in his sleep and Celestine patted his back gently. "I understand you perfectly. How could I not? I also left Philadelphia hoping to make a new life here in the west."

Elliott face became somber. "I also need to tell you that Parker told me he heard at the train depot that apart from the three who beat Joe, Crawford hired a gunslinger. It's amazing that in 1887 there are still people who live by the gun, but as long as people like Crawford pay for their services, they'll keep doing it. It will be a nasty fight. Parker is willing to fight. Miller is older, so I'm not sure about him. His sons don't care to live on the ranch, and he might be willing to sell."

"I'm sorry that you have to go through this."

"Yes, it is what it is. What I want to tell you is that I don't force my own ranch hands to stay here to fight against Crawford. Look what happened to Joe. It's my fight and my life to risk. I don't want you in danger, Celestine. And it will be dangerous."

"Elliott Maitland, you gave me shelter when no one else would. Do you think I'm going to abandon you and run away? I can hold my own with a gun or a rifle. I am making it my fight too. I have a Christmas tree to decorate, a meal to cook, and Christmas to celebrate. No one will spoil this for me. Besides, where would I go?"

CHAPTER 9

The day was not too cold. Snow covered the ground, but the air was milder and it didn't freeze your breath. Elliott and the men were in the barn saddling the horses, getting ready to go on the range, and Celestine was humming an old carol and decorating the Christmas tree. The puppy was jumping playfully at her feet.

She had brought with her, carefully packed in her trunk, a few of the ornaments that had adorned the rich Christmas tree at home in Philadelphia and it had enchanted her childhood every December. First, she took out the Christmas angel. Climbing on a chair, she placed it on top of the tree. It was so beautiful and familiar that Celestine felt tears in her eyes, remembering the happy times when she was a little girl, looking in wonder at the angel, with its silvery wings, smiling in blessing from the top of the tree.

Books, a few pictures of her parents, and a few Christmas ornaments was all she had in her trunk. That is what she cherished most in life. Very few clothes. When she became a pauper overnight, she discovered that her beautiful pink and blue and gold velvet and silk dresses were unsuitable when applying for a job of governess or teacher. So she gave them all away, keeping only a few modest outfits.

The four glass ornaments she had packed carefully in boxes in her trunk were now glittering from the tree branches. She added some papier maché decorations made of paper and fabric, which Elliott had given her. They'd belonged to the previous owners of the house. They were crudely done, but homey, adding charm to the tree and surprisingly they blended in well with her expensive ornaments.

She was wondering if popcorn on a string would be a nice addition, when she heard shouts outside, "Riders coming."

Elliott, who was ready to ride away, dismounted and stepped on the porch to face the newcomers with his rifle in his hand. Celestine cracked the door open to peek outside.

When the riders came closer, she felt him relax

his stance.

"It's Miller," he said.

Miller dismounted and came to shake hands with Elliott, who invited him inside.

"Ah, Miss Tillman, we meet at last," Miller said and after shaking her hand, he declined the invitation to come in the parlor. He went closer to the stove to warm up. "Nice tree. I don't think Maitland ever bothered to put one up before."

"A rancher doesn't have time for such...," Elliott grumbled.

"True," Miller agreed. He sniffed the air. "Nice vanilla smell. It reminds me of my grandma, who made a great pudding."

"It's the apple pie, but it's not ready. Please sit down and I'll pour coffee with biscuits, freshly made this morning and mulberry jam," Celestine invited him politely, wondering if he had come to inform her that she had no teaching job.

"Don't mind if I do." Miller took a seat at the kitchen table and accepted gratefully a cup of hot coffee.

Celestine knew by now that coffee was the cowboys' beverage of choice. Trying to tempt them with her favorite tea was pointless. She watched Miller devouring three of her biscuits, spreading generously the mulberry jam from the mercantile. She hoped that he would be less inclined to fire her after eating her fare.

"Well, Miss Tillman, you know your way around the kitchen. I was not sure, you coming from Philadelphia with such fancy credentials, Portman's Private School for Young Ladies for higher education and deportment. Do they teach you there how to fight in front of the saloon?" he asked, but his eyes were twinkling with humor.

"We don't have saloons in Philadelphia," Celestine answered with dignity.

Miller threw his head back and roared with laughter. "So, I guess you improvised what to do in such a novel place." And he laughed again. "Look, we have to talk. The virtuous ladies in this town have some objections to your increasing notoriety. Living here with Maitland is not exactly proper, but he assured me he was sleeping with his men in the bunkhouse and I believe him. There is no better alternative. The hotels are full, the boarding houses the same, and the teacher's cottage is not ready yet. Being close to Christmas, no soul in town has time to work on it. Therefore, I'm prepared to overlook the unusual living arrangements."

"Because you don't have a choice, you old coot. You need a teacher and it's the middle of the school year," Elliott scoffed.

"That too, I admit," Miller agreed. "Unlike my wife, I'm more practical. My question is, are you going to be a reliable teacher or are you going to get married quickly? Because considering your cooking abilities, you'll have offers aplenty."

Celestine thought about this. Of course, she intended to get married. If the right man proposed. "I don't know what the future will bring, but I can promise you that I'll honor the contract we signed and I hope you'll do the same. I'll be your teacher until the end of the school year in summer."

Miller beamed at her. "Good enough for me.

Also… if you could refrain from hitting men with your reticule and from threatening them with a gun, at least while in town."

"If men refrain from beating each other senseless, then yes, of course."

"Good. We have a deal." He turned to Elliott. "About Crawford, we have a problem. He hired men including a gunfighter and he is decided to chase us from our land. He made me an offer not even a quarter of the land's worth."

"What about your bull?"

"I think he gave him some sort of poisonous food. How? I don't know. I'd hate to think one of my men was in cahoots with Crawford. But how else could he have gotten to my bull? I'm a good rancher and I love this land, but my two eldest sons left for mining in Colorado and the others are younger."

"What about Johnny?"

"Johnny loves horses, but cattle not so much. He is interested in raising horses."

"Not a bad business if you want to expand."

"Are you kidding? I can barely make it with the cattle business. Anyhow, if Crawford kills my bull I'm finished and I can't place my family in danger fighting with him. I'm not as young as you or Parker."

"Are you going to let Crawford win?"

"No, I'm not going to sell to him. His offer was so low that it was offensive and it wouldn't cover my debts to the bank. But if I have at least a decent offer, then yes, I'll consider selling."

"I'm sorry to hear. You've been a great neighbor, Miller."

They shook hands and Miller left.

Elliott looked at Celestine. "I'm afraid it's just Parker and I against Crawford."

She came closer and placed her hand on his arm. "And me. I'm in this fight too."

Her golden-brown eyes were warm and luminous. Elliott felt himself drawn to their warm glow. He cupped her face and touched her lips with his own. The touch ignited a fire deep within him and he deepened the kiss.

"Boss." The door opened and Frank stuck his

head inside. Seeing the couple together, he smiled and pulled the door shut. "We are riding with the hay," he announced loudly from the porch.

Reluctantly, Elliott released the woman in his arms. "If Miller saw me, he'd have me hung."

Celestine was dazed by the kiss too. Of course, Richard had smacked her lips sometimes, but it was wet and unpleasant. Elliott tasted of mint and his touch had been magic. She wanted the kiss to never end, and to explore this new feeling further. Maybe she had low morals as the ladies said.

"Will you be all right here alone, Celestine," Elliott asked her, torn between the desire to stay with her and the work he had to do.

"Of course. Go. I'll be fine," she assured him.

Long after the men had gone, Celestine remained at the window, looking at the white landscape until the men disappeared in the distance. Sighing, she turned back to her cooking.

After she placed the roast beef in the oven, she looked at the beautiful tree and decided to make a popcorn string. She looked out the window again and cried in surprise and fear. There, pressed against the glass, was the distorted face of an Indian. She stepped back, her hand at her chest to calm down her rapid heartbeats. Had she locked the door like Elliott said? No, she was busy dreaming of his kiss.

She approached the door slowly. It was unlocked. She touched the latch, but the door was pushed open and she came face to face with the frightening Indian. Wait a minute! This was 1887, and Indians had not been on the warpath for a long time. But maybe this one didn't know about that.

"Four Fingers?" he asked.

"Out, on the range with the cattle," she answered, carefully taking her Derringer from her pocket.

He nodded. "Food?" he pointed at the stove.

Ah, if it was food he wanted, Celestine would feed him. Their cook always said that no soul in the world should go to bed hungry. Maybe the poor man was hungry. She fried some chicken and with leftover mashed potatoes placed them in front of him on the table. He was waiting patiently at the table, examining the Christmas tree with curiosity.

"Do you...," Celestine pointed at him, "...coffee?"

He blinked. "You don't speak English?" he asked, biting with relish in the succulent chicken leg.

"Of course I speak English," Celestine replied with indignation. "I'm a teacher. It was you who came in speaking in short words."

He shrugged. "Why waste time with a long speech? Besides, you were so frightened I thought you were ready to jump through the window."

"What did you expect? You just burst in without knocking on the door."

"Why waste time..."

"...knocking on the door."

"Maitland knows me. I'm Four Fingers' cousin. I helped him round up the cattle when he first moved in," he explained. "Bald Eagle, that's me. But they call me Tom."

"Tom Bald Eagle. Nice name."

"Yeah, they thought I would soar up like an eagle, but no such luck. I heard back east people are building all sorts of contraptions hoping to fly with them."

"I don't know. But I wouldn't be surprised," Celestine said. "Look at the trains. What a marvelous invention."

"Hmm. For a while, I ran shotgun for the stagecoach from Cheyenne to Deadwood, South Dakota. A rough town. I heard soon the stagecoach will be replaced by the train."

"It's called progress. By the way, I'm Celestine Tillman," she said looking at him polishing the last of his food. She cut him a good slice of apple pie.

"I know. I helped Four Fingers cut down your tree. Strange habit to move the tree inside the house. It looks nice though."

"We like to celebrate Christmas. When the tree is decorated like this, it brings the joy of Christmas into our hearts."

Bald Eagle swallowed the first bite of pie and

rolled his eyes with pleasure. "Good cook. Maitland is a lucky man."

Celestine blushed flustered. "We're not…. Mr. Maitland and I, we're not anything. I'm a teacher."

Bald Eagle raised an eyebrow as if saying 'Who are you fooling?' and continued eating his pie. "Anyway, tell your man that I saw Crawford meeting with one of Maitland's ranch hands. I suspect he knows, but just in case, tell him."

It took a moment for Celestine to understand. "You don't mean one of these nice men is a traitor."

"A planted mole. Yes, that's exactly what I mean." Bald Eagle nodded emphatically.

"But that is outrageous. Why would people do such things?"

"For money." Bald Eagle pushed the empty plate away and rose. "I'll be back when I can. Thank you for the food."

CHAPTER 10

It was the middle of the night when Celestine felt a wet nose against her hand. Awakened and disoriented, she looked down on the bed. "Oh, it's you, Puppy. What? You had a nightmare and couldn't sleep?"

But the dog whined and jumped off the bed, running straight to the door.

"You want outside at this hour? Nobody goes to the privy in the middle of the night," Celestine told him. She placed a wrap around her shoulders and her feet in her slippers and went to open the door for him to let him out. At least he was house broken and knew to ask to be let out. She opened the door and he ran outside. "Do your business and come back fast. It's cold."

But the little dog ran to the barn barking.

The silly dog will wake up the men, Celestine thought, only to see the dog growling and pulling at a man's boots. The man tried to balance a lantern in his hand and to shake his leg to get rid of the dog.

She just knew even without seeing his face that

he was not one of the ranch hands. Without thinking twice, Celestine grabbed the broom with long stick that rested near the door and ran outside. Busy with the dog, the man didn't see what fury came and whacked him on the head.

"What do you think you're doing? Leave my dog alone," Celestine cried at him, continuing to hit him with the broom, while the little dog bit him on the ankle.

Awaken by the noise, the ranch hands ran outside the bunkhouse in various state of undress to see what all the ruckus was about.

The stranger dropped the lantern and pulled out a gun. Another strike with the broom made the gun fire and the bullet went astray in the wall of the barn.

"Drop the gun," Elliott ordered pointing the Winchester at the intruder.

The man looked around and saw he was surrounded. A last whack of the broom made him drop his gun. "Call off your dog, mister."

The ranch hands jumped on him, found two other guns and a long knife, and tied him to a post in the barn.

"Celestine, what are you doing fighting with a broom against a fully armed intruder? You're going to give me white hair before my time," Elliott said, taking her into his arms because she was shaking.

"I had the Derringer in my pocket too, just in case, but I had no time to use it," she replied. "I sleep with it under my pillow."

"It's a good thing that you do."

"I thought he wanted to set the barn on fire," she explained, nestling closer to his warmth.

"That was probably his intention." Elliott looked over her head at Frank who shook his head. "He's not talking."

"What are you going to do? He could have been sent by Crawford."

"Yes, I know. I'll take him to the sheriff in town tomorrow. If he's not talking, the sheriff will keep him in jail a couple of days and then release him."

"But he tried to set the barn on fire," Celestine protested.

"Except that he didn't because we caught him

early. By the way, what woke you up?"

"The puppy whined that he wanted out. I think he heard the intruder," she explained, looking around for the puppy. The little dog, his mission accomplished, was waiting for her near the door ready to go inside, where it was warm. "He needs a name."

"Catcher or Guardian," Elliott suggested.

Frank came out of the barn. "He's not talking, but he'd have burned the barn with the animals inside if the little lion there had not heard him."

"Lion, Leo," Celestine said. "We'll take him tomorrow to town with us."

"With us?" Elliott didn't plan to take Celestine with him and the intruder. If the entire town saw them together, then people would start talking again.

"Let's go catch a few more hours of sleep. Tomorrow is another work day," Frank said. Good advice.

In the end, next day, Celestine had to leave the newly baptized Leo at home. Elliott reluctantly agreed to take her, but the idea of chasing through town after the energetic puppy was too much.

After breakfast, Celestine said good bye to her beloved puppy and climbed in the wagon seat near Elliott. In the back, the intruder was tied up and secured to the wagon, so he couldn't escape.

The day was pleasant, not frosty, although from time to time a wind gust made Celestine gather the blanket more tightly around herself.

"Beautiful land. Open space as far as you can see," Celestine observed.

"In the beginning, I missed the crowds and the wealth of trees from Virginia. Now, this is home. The narrow streets and busy cities of the east would make me itch. I like my space and my freedom here."

She smiled with understanding and turned to him to answer. At the corner of her eye, she perceived movement behind them. "Elliott," she cried out a warning. She caught the reins dropped by Elliott, just as a knife grazed his shoulder. He grabbed the assaulting hand and he pushed the other man back in the wagon.

Never letting go of the other man's wrist he twisted his arm behind his back and forced him to drop the knife.

Celestine stopped the wagon and jumped in the back to help Elliott. The ties had been cut, but there was enough rope to tie both his hands behind him and to the wagon.

Elliott looked at the sharp, long knife. If Celestine's warning had come a second later, he'd be dead.

"Where did he get the knife?" Celestine asked.

"Someone on my ranch gave it to him."

Celestine covered her mouth with her hand. "Oh, dear. Bald Eagle was right when he said we have a spy among us. I was hoping he was wrong."

"I've known for quite some time," Elliott confirmed, looking somberly at the knife.

"Do you know who he is?"

"I can guess. The only one I trust one hundred per cent is Four Fingers. He was with me from the beginning and saved my life countless times. The rest…"

"Did he cut you?" Celestine asked, examining

Elliott's shoulder.

"It's only a scratch. Too bad he cut my coat. I can sew it, but it won't be like new."

"Emily can do a good job."

"Emily?"

"You know, Emily Parker is the seamstress in town."

"Ah, Emily who was married to John's cousin, Fred. The Parkers don't talk to her. I'm not sure why, considering Fred died in some other woman's bed."

It had been just one hour since they had left the ranch. The first houses in Laramie could be seen in the distance. "Do you know Emily has electric light in her store? She signed up last year and swears it is the best investment she's made. Not only do they give more light than gas lamps, but they don't produce smoke and that characteristic gas odor that permeated her new dresses when she worked at night."

"Yes, the electric plant was built last year, but it will be some time until the remote ranches benefit too."

"In Philadelphia, electricity was introduced six

years ago in 1881. Don't we live in such a great time with all these new inventions?"

They stopped the wagon in front of Sam's mercantile, where Elliott left Celestine, and then he continued to the sheriff's office. He was lucky to find Bill Monroe in his office. He hauled the intruder down from the wagon and inside the office.

Monroe who was looking at some Wanted posters, leaned back in his chair. "What did you bring me, Maitland?"

"A night bird that almost burned down my barn. Does he look familiar?

Monroe studied the man, then shook his head.

"Nope. He's not Wanted…yet. Let me put him in jail and then we'll talk." He pushed the man in one of the two empty cells and locked it carefully without paying attention to his vocal protests that he was innocent. He returned in the front office. "Now, tell me what happened."

"Celestine's new dog alerted her that he wanted out and then he latched onto the intruder's leg until we came out to catch him. Of course, Celestine was bashing the man in the head with the broom."

The sheriff smiled. "Of course. The resourceful Miss Tillman. No offense meant," he added raising his hand up at the dark look Elliott gave him. "Any people or livestock killed, injured, stolen, or damaged in any way?"

"No. As I said, we were alerted in time to prevent any damage."

"Any property, buildings, objects, guns stolen, destroyed and such?"

"No."

"You were lucky. Sort of. You know, if no crime was committed, then it's just your word against his. He said he got lost in the middle of the night and stumbled onto your ranch when you grabbed him."

"He was walking on foot, in the dead of winter, in the middle of the night, with only a gas lantern with him, right near my barn."

"No horse?"

"Nope. But we found fresh tracks from two horses farther away. Whoever was there, left when he realized his partner in nightwalking was not returning."

Monroe looked into his empty coffee cup. "Unfortunately, even if I present him to the judge, without a definite crime, he'll be free. All I can do for you is to keep him in for three days."

Elliott nodded. He had three days to catch the real culprit who'd hired the intruder. It was not much, but it was better than if he walked away free right now. "Thanks."

Sheriff Monroe bent closer. "I tell you, Maitland, when I took this job, I didn't imagine that all people in this town are saints, but to plot arson and cattle poisoning this close to Christmas makes you wonder what kind of a man would do this. Don't underestimate him or the danger. Take care."

Elliott saluted and turned to leave, when the sheriff's voice stopped him. "Give my regards to the enterprising Miss Tillman and please keep her away from the saloon and out of trouble, will you?"

CHAPTER 11

Celestine looked after the wagon Elliott was driving, turning left at the next corner and disappearing from sight. She entered the mercantile, but Sam was busy attending other customers, so after browsing through the store, she left and walked slowly on the boardwalk, looking at the new buildings around.

The town was growing. It was not a one street town. Fancy new stores sprouted overnight. Some of them had electric lights provided by the electric plant, built last year in 1886. Sam would need to make improvements to his old store if he wanted to compete with the new Trabing Commercial Company, a larger store, who offered not only a variety of merchandise, but was also designed to attract and please the customers.

Celestine stopped in front of the dressmaker's store and admired one more time the elegant blue dress in the window. It would make any store in Philadelphia proud. She was hoping her new friend, Emily, might have some remnants of ribbons or fabric she could use to embellish the gifts she wrapped in plain coarse paper from the mercantile. The tree could also use colorful bows to cheer it up.

She opened the door and her attention was drawn to the drama unfolding inside. The haughty banker's wife, Cora Lynn Turner, was shouting at the top of her lungs at Emily, shaking a newly made dress in front of her.

"This is unacceptable. You promised it would be ready for Christmas."

Emily was trying to keep her composure, although her voice trembled and she had tears at the corners of her eyes. "I did my best and I worked nights. You wanted to change the lace."

"This lace is horrible. I can't wear this. You should have…"

"Belgian lace has to be special ordered. I can't help it if the shipping takes two weeks," Emily explained.

"Two weeks?" Cora Lynn shrieked. "That will be past New Year. Too late for me to wear it at any party.

Why don't you have quality lace available in your store?"

"Because it's very expensive and my clientele likes the one I have at the price I ask for the dresses. Not much demand for Belgian lace for a barn dance."

Cora Lynn stomped her foot. "I have to have Belgian lace. This won't do." And she lifted the dress again and tore the lace-bordered bodice.

"What have you done?" Emily cried aghast. "You destroyed my work. You have to pay for it."

"No, I won't pay for a dress for which I have no use."

"You have to pay or I'll complain to the judge."

Cora Lynn turned an unbecoming shade of red. "You... you... merchant girl, you wouldn't dare..." And she slapped Emily on the face.

It was more than Celestine could bear. She grabbed Cora Lynn's hand and pushed her away. "Don't you dare hit Emily. You arrogant woman."

The push made Cora Lynn land in a chair that was behind her. Unfortunately, the bouncing movement made the majestic hat, covered by flowers and ostrich feathers, fall off her head to the ground, taking with it the artfully arranged curls at the back of her head that apparently were more attached to the hat than to her own head. Cora Lynn started to emit lugubrious howls. Her own hair was thin and gathered in a small knot on top of her head.

Despite her red cheek, Emily giggled at the sight and covered her mouth with her hand.

Celestine was aware that through the open door, the noise had attracted a crowd who was enjoying the fight inside and commenting. Mostly in a positive way – she observed relieved.

"…she didn't want to pay…," a gentleman with a cigar explained to the people not so close to the entrance who were asking what happened.

"…and she's a banker's wife. For shame," added a stout matron. "She slapped the seamstress. Lucky the new teacher was able to stop her."

"What do you know, her hair fell off her head." Snickers and laughter were heard in the crowd.

Cora Lynn looked to the ground with horror and realized her predicament was worse than she thought. "I'll kill you," she said and jumped at Celestine.

"Cat fight," announced a cowboy, slapping his hat to a post with glee.

At that moment, Elliott turned his wagon onto the street and saw the crowd in front of the dressmaker's store. He had a premonition. What were the odds that his prim schoolteacher was in the middle of a fracas again? Vaulting over the railing at the edge of the wooden boardwalk, he pushed people aside and went inside the store just in time to prevent the banker's wife from completely tearing off the sleeve from Celestine's coat. All three delicate women were shrieking in a deafening chorus and attempting to hit the one another past Elliott.

"What is going on here?" Sheriff Monroe's voice was heard outside. It seemed the good sheriff had a premonition too, and had followed Elliott to the dressmaker's.

The sheriff made his way in. "Ah, Miss Tillman, why am I not surprised to see you here?"

Celestine looked with dismay at her sleeve.

"Perhaps because I'm Emily's friend," she muttered.

Cora Lynn Turner fell back prostrate in the chair.

"This person of low morals assaulted me. Arrest her,
Sheriff."

"I pushed her away after she slapped Emily,"
Celestine protested.

The sheriff looked at Emily's red cheek, hmm-ed
to himself, and picked up the hat from the floor. He
straightened some feathers and shook the curls, then,
unfazed, he handed it to the banker's wife. "I believe this
is yours, ma'am."

Cora Lynn snatched it and placed it on her head,
somewhat askew with the curls bouncing over her left
ear.

"She wouldn't pay for the dress she ordered,"
Celestine said.

"I'm not going to pay for a dress I'm not going to
wear," Cora Lynn argued.

The sheriff raised his eyes to the ceiling. Give
him a saloon full of unruly cowboys instead, and he

could deal with them better. "Ma'am, did you order the
dress?"

"Yes, I did. I wanted to wear it for Christmas and
she..." She pointed at Emily. "...can't make it before the
year is over."

"That's because she changed her mind and
wanted Belgian lace. I have to special order that and it
won't come any sooner than two weeks," Emily
explained, looking in dismay at the torn bodice. "You
know, Sheriff, I wouldn't ask for money if I could sell it
to another customer, but she tore the dress apart in a fit of
nerves."

"She should pay for Emily's work," Celestine
said loudly.

"The new teacher's right, she should pay,"
echoed someone outside.

"She's a banker's wife. She has money to pay,"
another voice agreed.

"Or maybe not, considering she's playing poker
above the saloon every week."

This new information created a flood of

comments and opinions outside, a loud protest from Cora Lynn, and new efforts on the sheriff's part to calm the spirits.

"Hoa, folks, I'm not a judge to dispense decisions about who's right and who's wrong. I'm a sheriff and I have to ensure order in this town. So, you all, outside the store, please disperse, there will be nothing else of importance going on here." He waited a few moments until the people in the street started moving away. Then he turned to Cora Lynn. "Mrs. Turner, please let me escort you back home and just consider that Mrs. Parker put a lot of time and effort in making your dress. This is the time of year when we should be charitable to our fellow human."

Opening the door for her, he motioned her out.

"Do you think she'll pay?" Celestine asked looking after them.

Emily's eyes hardened. "She'll pay. I'm going to her husband."

"I heard the banker is even more penny pincher than she is," Elliott warned her.

"Yes, he is. He'll be interested to know where his wife is spending money every week," Emily said, touching her still burning red cheek.

"Oh, Emily, what if it's not true?" Celestine asked.

"Then I suppose he'll want this untrue fact not to be spread around town. Now come here Celestine. Give me your coat to sew your sleeve."

"Ladies, could you assure me that if I go to the train depot to ask about a shipment, you will not turn this whole town upside down?" Elliott asked.

Later, when he returned, Elliott found Celestine and her friend drinking tea and pouring over a new fashion magazine. They invited him to have tea and tiny cucumber sandwiches, but Elliott wanted to return to the ranch before dark. He was hungry, but the tiny green sandwiches were not his idea of a meal.

They said good-bye to Emily and they were off. Elliott stopped the wagon in front of the hotel, and asked Celestine to wait for him a minute. He wanted to ask a question inside. She was shaken by the idea he was so put off by her unladylike behavior that he wanted to get rid of her and to find her a room at the hotel. The idea of spending Christmas alone in a hotel room was not appealing. And what about her Christmas tree that Four Fingers had brought and she had decorated with such love? How could she leave it behind? How could she leave the warm kitchen behind and what about her little dog? Were dogs allowed at the hotel?

She was debating all this and fighting the incoming tears of self-pity when Elliott returned frowning and started the wagon on the road north to the ranch, without saying anything.

Celestine supposed there were no rooms available, but after a while, she couldn't bear the silence any longer. "People in town think that I have low morals and today's dispute with the banker's wife confirmed their ill opinion of me, but I don't know what I could have done differently. She slapped Emily. I couldn't let it go without protesting."

He looked at her amused. "You certainly showed

your protest loud and clear, Celestine. The fact that two busybodies disapprove of you doesn't mean the entire town does. Today, for instance, they were on your side wholeheartedly."

"You think so?"

He nodded. "Yes. It's just that for such a prim and proper schoolteacher, trouble finds you every time you go to town."

She sniffed. "But you wanted to find me a room at the hotel. I am an unwelcome guest at your house."

What was she talking about? Women had a convoluted way of thinking and they twisted reality in such way... Elliott thought. "What are you talking about? Why do you feel unwelcome in my house?"

"You looked for a room at the hotel for me right now. Don't deny it."

"I did no such thing."

"Then why did you stop at the hotel?"

After a moment of hesitation, looking straight ahead, Elliott answered, "To ask if a certain person had made a reservation for Christmas Eve and if indeed they have a room reserved under his name."

"Who?"

"Orville Maitland, my brother."

CHAPTER 12

"The station master at the depot gave me this letter. It came a few days ago." Elliott searched his pocket and gave Celestine a folded piece of paper. "Read it."

"Dear Elliott,..."

"He never called me dear in his life and we were never close and never had the same friends, never played together as boys do. It was not a big difference in age, only four years. We were different. He was always with his nose in a book and praised by my father, while I was a rambunctious little boy and later teenager, always in trouble. The black sheep of the family," Elliott explained. "The more my father tried to make me fit the mold of my brother, the more I rebelled. I was not rebellious by nature, but the constant disapproval made me do the opposite than what he wanted."

"After you left, Mama fell into a decline. She blamed us for chasing you

away. After a lot of thinking, I realized that we had done exactly that. But it was too late to change anything. I had no idea where you were. Mama died three months after you left. I think she lost the will to live... Oh, poor lady. She missed you so much," Celestine said, wiping her eyes.

"She never showed in any way that she disagreed with my father. She never protested his harsh punishments."

"You forget that she was from a different generation. She was taught that women needed to show respect and obedience to their husbands."

"Different generation or not, I bet in her place you would have given him a piece of your mind. And if that didn't work, you'd have taken out your Derringer to make him stop using his belt on your child," he said half joking, half meaning it.

Celestine blinked. "He used the belt on you? I'd have scratched his eyes out," she said dead serious. The idea that an adult could use a belt on a defenseless child, on any child, not only her own, made her blood boil with anger. She looked back at the letter. *"At the time, I was engaged to Joanna Stone - remember the freckled redhead from the neighborhood? Joanna and I were married in a quiet ceremony a month later with only our family in attendance. A year later, Joanna gave birth to a beautiful baby girl. Annabelle was tiny, with a mop of red hair like her mother, and I fell in love instantly. To my surprise, Papa didn't share my feelings. He wanted an heir for his apothecary empire. In his mind, Joanna failed to give him that. He was so obsessed that he ignored Annabelle completely and he started to be rude and to put down Joanna for what he perceived as a failure. He was surprised when not only did I disagree with him, but also I warned him that if he continued his rude behavior, I would take my family and make a new life away from Virginia...."*

Celestine paused, thinking how different her own father had been, and how he encouraged her to be herself and stand up in life. It was like he predicted that she'd be alone and would need a lot of strength and courage to survive, a woman alone in the world.

She looked back at the letter in her hand. *"It was about that time that I hired a Pinkerton agent to find where you were. I thought you went to California to work at a bank, like you did here. Imagine my surprise to find out that you were a rancher in Wyoming. My relationship with Papa continued to deteriorate. Joanna was pregnant again, so he stopped berating her, but he decided to borrow a lot of money to buy another apothecary in Maryland. It was a risky business and we had a big fight about it. Of course, he did what he wanted and ignored my opinion. I realized that the apothecary was his dream, not mine, and I started to become detached and look for a way out. Unfortunately, it all happened sooner than I thought. One day, Papa went to inspect one of the stores and had a fight with the clerk there. He came home angry, locked himself in his office, and a couple of hours later we heard a hoarse cry. I forced the door open, but he was already gone. The doctor said apoplexy is common for men his age....."* Celestine looked at Elliott. "Oh, Elliott, both your parents are dead. Had you known, would you have gone to your father's funeral?"

"No. Not only I didn't want to go, but also I'm sure he wouldn't have wanted me there. And a rancher can't take time off. Ranching is all year round, continuous work." His tone was categorical, but Celestine felt he was grieving for the mother that loved him, but had been too scared to disobey her husband, for the father that didn't approve of him and didn't love him, and finally for what if they all had been different, given a second chance. She placed her hand on his arm to give him comfort. He transferred the reins in one hand and with his free hand over hers, he squeezed gently.

"Come on, finish reading," he finally said.

"The entire funeral process was very stressful for Joanna and she went into labor early. It was a long and painful labor. In the end, the child, a boy, was stillborn. My poor Jo, my beacon in life, had lost so much blood that I felt life going out of her. I held her hand long after she

*died. What would I do now without my Jo?
I was sure that I'd die of a broken heart."*

Celestine wiped the tears from her cheeks. "Oh, the poor man. So many losses at the same time. Nobody deserves to suffer like that."

"You are a soft heart, my compassionate lioness," Elliott joked to hide his own deep emotion.

"I was agonizing every day, walking from room to room with Joanna's picture in hand, trying to recapture her presence, until one day when Annabelle pulled my hand, looked at me, and said, 'I'm hungry'. Then I realized that I couldn't cry and indulge in self pity. I had a child who needed me. Looking around me, I realized that the old house, full of memories, was suffocating me. I sold the apothecaries and the house. I kept a bare minimum of pictures and mementos and decided to

start a new life out west. I heard California has a dry climate. I don't know what I'd do there. Probably open a business. Who knows? Life is unpredictable as you've proven.

I would like to see you. I'll make a detour and I'll be in Laramie on December 24th, Christmas Eve. I already sent a telegram and reserved a room at the Grand Hotel. I'll stay there for three days. I hope you'll find it in your heart to forgive whatever wrong part I had in our estrangement and come to meet me and Annabelle.

I'll take the train west on December 27th

Your brother, Orville."

Celestine looked again over the letter, then folded

it carefully, and gave it back to Elliott. She was unusually quiet and Elliott wondered what she was thinking.

"This is embarrassing, but I don't have any money," she confessed. "I spent my last pennies buying licorice for the ranch hands."

"Why would you buy them licorice and what's the connection with my brother?" he asked dumbfounded.

"I made a little gift for everyone. It's Christmas. Every person, regardless of age, deserves to enjoy this day and to celebrate it properly. And now your brother is coming too. Such a wonderful surprise. We have food aplenty, but tomorrow is Christmas Eve. You have to buy gifts for them."

"Wait! I haven't even decided to meet with Orville. No point talking about Christmas or gifts." Elliott was taken aback by the rapid pace at which Celestine was moving along.

"Of course you'll meet him. If not, then he'll go west and you'll never see him again."

"That was what we agreed upon when I left Virginia."

She looked at him aghast. "That was five years ago. You changed, and he did too. Life is different now for both of you. It's an opportunity to reconnect with your brother. If you don't, then you'll be sorry later."

"You might be right, but you have such a tendency to take charge over..."

"Oh." Just this one sound and she bit her lower lip, a sign she was worried or distressed. "Yes, I... I'm sorry. I tend to do that. Take over things.... It's just that I thought this year I'd spend Christmas alone and I was so happy to be at the ranch and have people around me and ...I guess I took over the preparations. You don't want me in the middle of your family."

"What are you talking about? Of course, I want you there. You are more family to me than Orville is because I got to know you, while he is practically a stranger to me. As for the preparations, go ahead and do whatever you want. All the men are talking about what you cooked for dinner and what Christmas delights you will surprise us with."

It was true, Elliott thought. In such a short time, Celestine had become vital to the ranch, not only for the good food she prepared, but also for the warmth she projected and the love she spread all around her.

"All right then. I'm glad. I might not have a teaching position after antagonizing the banker's wife today, but I'm not going to think about it. I'll let myself enjoy a Christmas among good people and the future will take care of itself."

"You'll have the job because Miller promised you. The banker's wife has no say in it. Neither her, nor Miller's wife. What they will do for sure is that they'll try to ostracize you, to keep you away from what they consider the high society in Laramie. Are you tough enough to endure such treatment from the mighty local ladies?"

"Of course. I've endured much worse at the hands of the Philadelphia society. I concluded that I truly don't care what a bunch of stuffy women think or talk about me. Besides, I already have real friends here that matter to me. Prudence Parker, Emily, Sam. And then there are the nice people, who are not influenced by gossip, Dr. Pendergast, the pastor, and Sheriff Monroe, and I'm sure many others like them."

Elliott stopped the wagon in front of the barn and the little dog came running to meet Celestine.

CHAPTER 13

It was Christmas Eve in the morning.

The men declared the decorated Christmas tree to be the most beautiful they had ever seen. Celestine wondered how many trees if any, they had seen, and how many family Christmases they had celebrated. She was determined to make a happy day for all of them including the guests that arrived just in time to spend this joyous day together with them.

But first she had another gift to wrap. She took out of her trunk a small box and opened it. Inside she kept the pearl earrings she had received from her mother. The box was a pretty rosewood, hand carved, with a decorated top and mother of pearl inlay. She'd seen it in a window shop when she was a little girl and she liked it very much. Her father had bought it for her. The bottom was padded and covered with velvet. She kept her mother's earrings in it, but it would serve as a very beautiful pincushion.

Celestine knew just the person who could use it.

Later, that morning, the wagon stopped in front of the dressmaker's store. Celestine went in to say Merry Christmas to her friend, while Elliott continued to the train depot to ask when the Union Pacific express train would arrive from Cheyenne. He waited a moment longer to see that Celestine did not meet with any trouble. Everything was quiet, and there were no other ladies there. Reassured, Elliott urged the horses to the train depot.

Celestine entered the store and found her friend hard at work, at the sewing machine. "Hey, Emily, it's Christmas Eve. You could take a break." She took a seat in one of the elegant Victorian chairs provided for the patrons of the store.

Emily raised her eyes from the deep red silk she was sewing. "I have to finish this dress for tomorrow. It's for one of the girls from the saloon."

"I bet Mrs. Miller would object to you working for one of those girls," Celestine said, only half joking.

"Mrs. Miller has her husband to pay her bills, I

don't. Even when he was alive, Fred Parker seldom had two pennies to rub together. I had to scrimp and save and hide money from him to pay the bills. I have worked all my life for what I have. And so do the girls at the saloon. Most of them are very nice and they always pay me for what they order. Unlike other hoity-toity ladies I know."

"It's Christmas Eve, don't be upset." Celestine looked around. "Where is your tree?"

"I don't have one. But I plan to go upstairs to my room after I finish this dress. I have a cat and a comfortable chair. I'll make a cup of hot chocolate and indulge in one of the dime novels. When I bought the store, the room was filled with dime novels. I kept them and now they provide a welcome retreat."

Celestine extracted from her reticule the wrapped gift. "Here. Merry Christmas, Emily."

Emily blinked in surprise. "For me? I didn't expect anything. May I open it?"

"Tomorrow. It will be such a pleasant night, anticipating Christmas Day, opening gifts, going to church, and having a nice family dinner."

"I don't have any of that," Emily sighed. "I never did. I was an orphan. The Parkers think Fred was generous to marry me. In reality, my sewing was providing most of the money in the family."

Celestine touched her hand. "If I had a room of my own, I would invite you to spend Christmas together. As it is, not only am I living at Mr. Maitland's on sufferance, but also I don't have any money left and I'm not sure if I'll have a teaching position after the New Year."

"What are you going to do?"

"I'm trying not to think, hoping tomorrow will take care of itself. But I'm a good cook. Perhaps I could find a job... Besides, I know Mr. Maitland will not throw me out. He'll help me."

Cutting the fabric loose from the sewing machine, Emily looked at her. "Maitland is a good man. He doesn't waste his time drinking or playing poker at the saloon. Five years ago, when he bought the Barnett ranch, many girls had their eyes on him, including Cora Lynn Turner. She was not married to the banker then.

But Maitland let them know that the ranch is his first priority and the matchmakers left him in peace. No woman has lived in that bachelors' place ever. Until you. Perhaps that's why people in town have been so intrigued by your living there." Emily pointed to a bunch of colorful knitted scarves, artfully arranged on a round table nearby. "Let me give you a gift too. I intended to do it anyhow, after you defended me from Cora Lynn. Pick one of those. Whichever color you like."

"For me? You don't have to," Celestine objected. The scarves were beautiful and she had another dear person to gift. "They are lovely and so soft. I have never been good at knitting."

"I knit them in the evenings while I read. They sell well in winter. Which color do you want?"

"This dark blue. Thank you," Celestine accepted, marveling at the softness of the woolen scarf. "And I can just now tell you that I have a very dear person in mind and I had no idea what to give him. This is perfect. Thank you, Emily."

"You needed a gift for Mr. Maitland? I wondered

why you picked such a dark color."

"No, the gift is not for Elliott. I already have a nice thing for him. This is for Sam."

Emily paused while attaching the ribbon to the red dress and looked at Celestine. "Sam, who?"

"Sam, the owner of the mercantile."

"You mean, that old codger, who grumbles all the time and never has any nice words for the customers who enter his store?"

Celestine nodded. "The very one. Grumbling, he invited me inside his store when I was half frozen and I despaired that Mr. Miller had forgotten to meet me at the train depot. And then he convinced Elliott to take me to his ranch. Now, despite my uncertain future, I have a nice place to spend Christmas with kind people."

"I see. Here, take that golden one for yourself." Emily rose and deftly wrapped the dark blue one in paper and the gold one around Celestine's neck. "There. You look nice."

"Thank you, Emily. You are so generous."

Emily shook her head. "No, my dear. It's you

who gave me a precious and rare gift. Your friendship. The decent women in town are either married or young girls. The married ones keep together, talking about children, families, household problems, and recipes. The younger unmarried ones giggle together sharing silly unrealistic dreams about love. They all like to gossip. I am a strange bird among them. I was married, but now I work and earn my living. I can't talk about any of the subjects that are interesting to them and I refuse to spread gossip about my customers."

"I see. Then I'm glad to call you my friend because I was in desperate need of one too."

Meanwhile Elliott stopped his wagon near the train depot, and he saw the depot master coming out agitated.

"Could you tell me when the Union Pacific train will be arriving from Cheyenne?" Elliott asked him.

"That's the problem, Maitland. I got a telegram from Cheyenne that the train left on time. It was supposed to be here half an hour ago. There is no falling snow and the tracks are clear." The depot master was a portly man and the worry showed clearly on his florid face. "And to top it all, Cornell, that new guy who bought a ranch east of town, came by and told me that he rode to fix a fence this morning and he thinks he saw the train stopped beyond Indian Springs."

Elliott looked at him. "You think something fishy is going on?"

"I don't think, I know. Deep in here." He touched his barrel-like chest. "I feel it." He leaned closer. "I bet it is that outlaw, Jimmy Lamont, again. I called the sheriff."

The first thought that crossed Elliott's mind was that it was not an auspicious situation for meeting his brother. The second was that he needed a good horse to ride out there to see what had happened. He had horses harnessed to the wagon and no saddle.

"Ah, there he is," the depot master's words interrupted his thoughts.

Sheriff Monroe was dismounting near them, tying his horse to the railing. He saluted Elliott briefly and turned to the depot master. He asked a few questions about the location where the rancher saw the train.

"All right," he concluded. "I'm going."

"Wait, Sheriff," Elliott stopped him. "I'm coming with you. Give me five minutes to get a horse from the stables."

"I don't have time to wait, Maitland. And in general, I don't like posse-like expeditions. I am much faster and efficient when I go alone," the sheriff answered impatiently.

"I have to go. My brother and niece are on that train," Elliott explained with a hint of desperation in his voice.

The depot master interfered. "Take my horse, Maitland. It's behind the building. It doesn't look like much, but he has endurance."

Elliott thanked him and went to take the horse. The sheriff was right, time was of the essence. There, he found the young helper, Tommy, and asked him to run to the dressmaker to tell Miss Tillman to wait for him either there or at the depot where he'd left the wagon with his own horses.

The youngster looked at him with doubt. "I'll tell her. But you know Miss Tillman doesn't take well to orders," he answered scratching his head.

The horse was not going to win any races soon, but it was already saddled. When he joined the sheriff, he saw that Lloyd Richardson was there too and ready to go with them. Why? That was a mystery and Richardson was a rather quiet man. Elliott didn't mind people not talking as long as they minded their own business.

"Do you think it was Jimmy Lamont who stopped the train?" the sheriff asked the station master.

"Oh, it was Jimmy Lamont all right," a deep voice from behind answered. The newcomer was stout, mounted on a horse that was handled harshly and snorting loudly.

Elliott disliked him instantly and swore to keep his distance from the man whatever his interest was.

The man pulled roughly on the bridle to stop the horse from moving and continued, "Jimmy Lamont, wanted, $1500 reward." He waved a Wanted poster in his hand. "He's mine."

"You want to come with us?" Richardson asked.

"Nah, I work alone. Alone is best. Don't split the reward with anyone." Giving them a sardonic grin, showing two front teeth missing, he galloped away.

Sheriff Monroe smacked his lips with displeasure. "That was Murphy or Murdock, a bounty hunter. He never catches his prey. He shoots them dead. And then he collects the reward. Let's go."

CHAPTER 14

The train was indeed stopped on the tracks, the engine releasing steam in the frosty air, but not as much as if it had been fully working. Some big rocks were blocking the tracks, but the train's locomotive had stopped before hitting them and derailing. The sheriff, Elliott and Lloyd Richardson took shelter behind some boulders at a distance from the train.

"You know, I don't think it is Jimmy Lamont. He works alone and he does it quietly, threatening each passenger and relieving them of valuables as fast as possible. Then he jumps out and disappears. One man can't stop a train like that. Why would he?" Sheriff Monroe told the other two.

"Look," Richardson pointed far in the distance past the train. "One of them is leaving."

Elliott looked at the figure fast riding in the opposite direction. "That's the bounty hunter. I would know his horse anywhere."

The sheriff nodded his agreement. "The bounty

hunter discovered that his prey was not holding up the train. Now he's going back to Cheyenne."

"Why doesn't he hunt the gang on the train?"

"Because that's not how he operates. He follows one outlaw at a time and shoots him dead without warning. He's not going to fight the whole gang," the sheriff clarified.

"There is one robber on the roof," Elliott observed. "I wonder if he's watching for approaching riders like us or just passing from one car to the front of the train. I'm going after him."

Richardson nodded. "I'll try to surprise them from the rear."

"Then I'll go for the locomotive to see what stopped it. Maitland, did you say you have relatives on the train?"

"My brother and my four year old niece. I hope they are fine."

The sheriff nodded and looked at Richardson.

"I don't have anyone on the train. I was going after Lamont," Richardson answered. No details were supplied, and no one asked. His reasons were his own. That was the unwritten law of the west. No questions asked. People liked their privacy and almost everyone had secrets.

They were lucky this area had some brush and it was easy to get close to the train without being seen. Elliott reached the train and vaulted up between two cars. Then he climbed on top. The man was facing in the other direction and had a coal shovel in his hand. Elliott tried to be silent, but the man heard him and turned back to face him. He dropped the shovel and reached for his gun. Elliott threw himself at the man grabbing his wrist. The gun noise might alert the others inside and endanger the lives of the passengers.

They rolled closer to the edge and Elliott saw the shovel was within his reach on the roof where the other man had dropped it. He hit the other man under the chin with his fist, then grabbed the shovel. The man cried out and raised his gun. Elliott hit the armed hand. The gun fell to the ground and the man trying to catch it slid over the edge.

Elliott looked down. The man was not moving. But he heard noise in between the cars.

"Are you still there, Zeb?" he heard a man's voice. Elliott raised the shovel again and when a younger face showed up looking on the roof of the car, he hit it with all his force. The man fell between the cars.

Elliott wondered how many men were there. He was ready to descend when something glittered in the black coal dust on the roof of the car. It was a pretty gold locket on a chain. It had fallen from the robber while they were fighting. He pocketed it, intending to return it to the passenger from whom it had been stolen.

Assuring himself that the two robbers remained unmoving, Elliott picked up the shovel and carefully made his way down between the cars.

A gun shot sounded in the last car. Elliott opened the door and entered the car. A man was standing watching over the frightened passengers. Without hesitation, Elliott took advantage of his surprise and hit him with the shovel. The gun flew from the man's hand and he fell to the floor. Elliott picked up the gun.

"Could you guys tie him up?" He figured some of the passengers would act when awaken from stupor. He ran through the car and exited the other side. He entered the last car just in time to see Richardson exchanging gun fire with a man hidden behind the last seat.

"He has a hostage," Richardson cautioned him.

"Hold on to this," Elliott said and gave him the shovel.

"Why?"

"It comes handy," Elliott answered. He opened the door and went back outside. The door was peppered by bullets, but he hoped no one was hit. He climbed on top of the car and crawled on the roof until he reached the end of the car and of the train. Carefully he slid in the back and tried the door. It was locked. Usually, the last door was locked to prevent accidents. He raised his gun and fired straight into the lock. A good shove with his foot and the door opened.

Unfortunately, it was not a surprise and the outlaw was expecting him with his gun raised. He fired, but Elliott ducked out of sight. The outlaw held by the scruff a little boy. Instead of being scared, the kid bit him on the hand, distracting him. In that instant, Elliott grabbed the armed hand and twisted it until he dropped the gun. Elliott shoved it in the middle of the car.

Richardson came running and tied the outlaw's hands behind his back.

"Hold the fort here. I left one in the next car," Elliott told him.

Richardson laughed. "I'm a rancher, Maitland. I know how to rope a steer and he's not getting untied. Let's leave him here. I want to know what happened to the sheriff."

They made their way through the car and through the cries of relief from the passengers. A small child's voice called after them, "Hey, mister, wait for me."

The little boy ran after them. Richardson looked around, but no one claimed the child. He hunkered down and asked him. "Where are your parents, kid?"

"My Dad is in the other car and he must be scared."

"Listen boy, you'd better stay here. It is still

dangerous in the other cars," Elliott said.

"I'm not a boy," the child protested. Taking her cap off, she uncovered a wealth of red curls reaching to the middle of her back.

Richardson picked her up. "Let's go find your Dad."

She beamed at him and patted his cheek. "I like you. Can I marry you, when I'll be grown-up?" she asked impishly.

Richardson almost stumbled over the railing between cars. "I'll be an old man by then."

Elliott opened the door to the next car cautiously, but it was calm inside. The robber was on the floor all tied up and with a handkerchief over his mouth.

"He was talking filthy," one of the ladies explained.

"Daddy," the little girl cried and Richardson set her down.

A tall gentleman with round glasses rose from his seat. "Annabelle, where did you go?"

Elliott came closer, looking at the man. "Hello,

.

Orville. What a way to meet after all these years."

"You're right. I imagined a peaceful day at the hotel, telling each other what happened, reconnecting. And instead... this. Not to mention I was immersed in a book and I didn't realize Annabelle had disappeared. Where was she?"

Elliott laughed. "You don't want to know, but you'll have your hands full with her. Now I have to go, but I'll be back."

He ran after Richardson.

They found the sheriff in the car near the locomotive, the express car, talking with the fireman. The engineer was dazed by a hit on the head from one of the robbers. The last two robbers had been subdued by the sheriff.

"They were lucky to see the rocks blocking the tracks or at this speed the locomotive and the cars could have derailed and passengers hurt," the sheriff explained.

"They wanted the code to the safe box," the fireman said. "The engineer said he doesn't have it and that only at the destination the man in charge from the

Union Pacific Express Company can open it. They hit him. When the sheriff came in, they were trying to open it and talking about blowing it up with dynamite."

"Did they rob the passengers?" the sheriff asked.

"Yes, they did," Richardson answered.

The sheriff nodded. "Let's round them up first. These two are tied up. How many are there?"

"There are two tied up in the last two cars, and the one on the roof fell down. I don't think he'll be able to run away anytime soon, but he's not tied. And one fell between cars. I had no time to tie him up. Six in all," Elliott counted.

"Let's bring the others here, tie them all up, and empty their pockets of what they stole from the passengers," Sheriff Monroe said. "Did you find your brother?" he asked Elliott.

"Yes, I did. And my niece," Elliott smiled, remembering what a handful his tiny niece was.

They found the tied robbers where they'd left them, and brought them cursing and kicking into the express car. The sheriff remained with them while Elliott and Richardson went to look for the last two. The one who fell from the roof was still not moving. They couldn't find the other one. Maitland bent down to look under the cars and this saved his life because a shot exploded right where he was standing.

He dropped to the ground and looked past the ditch that bordered the tracks. The sun blinded him, so he rolled inside the tracks under the train. Yes, there was a faint glint in the brush on the other side of the ditch. He took his time and when he saw another glint through the brush, he fired.

There was silence for a few long minutes. Then, he heard a faint noise and departing horses in the distance. Ah, one of the robbers had escaped. Too bad. These men should be brought to justice so that regular citizens could travel by train in peace. It was 1887. The time of the Wild West was long gone. Okay, maybe not so long, but it was gone nevertheless.

"Are you wounded?" Richardson's voice sounded near him.

"I'm fine. But one of them escaped," Elliott told

him, rolling out from under the train and getting up.

"Too bad. Sheriff Monroe will have to form a posse to go after him," Richardson answered, dusting his clothes off.

CHAPTER 15

They found the sheriff writing a detailed inventory of the money and valuables recovered from the robbers. Then he placed it all in a satchel.

"The passengers can come to reclaim them from my office," he said satisfied.

"Sorry, Sheriff, one of them escaped," Maitland told him.

"I'm pleased we caught the others, the passengers are unharmed, and most of the stolen stuff is here, if not all. I thank you both for your help and I will ask you to ride back to the depot and tell the depot master to send a crew to remove the rocks from the tracks. I'll wait here with the rest of them."

Maitland urged Richardson to return fast to the Laramie train depot and he went to see his brother. He found Orville holding his daughter in his arms. "She is desolate because one of the robbers yanked from her neck the locket with her mother's picture," he explained.

Elliott slapped his forehead. "I forgot about the

locket one of the robbers dropped. I have to give it to the sheriff." He pulled out of his pocket a delicate locket on a gold chain with intricate engravings.

"Mama's locket," Annabel exclaimed and clapped her hands.

"It has Joanna's picture inside," Orville added.

Elliott opened it and inside there was the picture of their neighbor's redhead, freckled daughter turned into a beautiful woman looking at him with a hint of sadness in her eyes. "Here you go, kid," he said and placed it around Annabelle's neck. "Now I have to ride back to inform the depot master what happened and to bring a crew to remove the rocks from the tracks. I'll see you back in Laramie."

"Elliott, I hate to impose, but is there any way we could ride back with you? I have only a small portmanteau. The trunk can be left at the station. Annabelle is cold and tired."

Elliott thought about it. By now, Richardson was close to Laramie, so carrying the news to town had been accomplished. The station master's horse was sturdy and enduring. It could carry two. It would take them longer, but they'd be in Laramie before the train for sure. There was also the sheriff's horse, but he hated to leave Bill Monroe without a horse here in the middle of nowhere. The depot master's horse would do. "Let's try it."

The gelding didn't object when Orville mounted in the saddle behind Elliott who was holding Annabelle wrapped in a blanket. He just plodded on going back to town. Somewhere close to the depot they met the crew on their way to clear the tracks.

Earlier, when the young man working at the depot came to inform Celestine that Elliott went riding with the sheriff to see what had happened to the train, her breath got caught in her throat with fear. What if there were outlaws who'd stopped the train? She realized she'd spoken out loud when the man answered.

"Probably they are outlaws if they stopped the train. The sheriff thought it might be Jimmy Lamont, but he never stops the train. He works alone, you see. This time it's a gang for sure."

This explanation increased her fear. Elliott was brave and ready to fight, but he was a rancher, not a gunfighter or sheriff. Guessing her thoughts, the young clerk said, "Don't worry, ma'am. Mr. Maitland can hold his own with the roughest robbers around. He helped Sheriff Monroe several times in the past. Why, it was just last month that he drew faster than a cheating card player at the saloon who had a dispute with one of the younger Miller boys."

The thought that Elliott was in danger frequently made Celestine shiver. Train robbers? He could be wounded or even killed. The world without him would be so sad. How had he become so important to her and in such a short time? She wanted to be strong. She'd lost her parents and everything she'd had. She was alone in the world, and had sworn not to become attached to another human being and look what she had done... She'd fallen in love with Elliott Maitland, gruff rancher that he was. He hid a generous nature inside and he was a hard-working man, fair and honest...

"Ma'am..." Tommy, the young clerk interrupted

her thoughts. "Mr. Maitland said you have to wait for him either here at the dressmaker's or at the train depot."

"I'm coming to the depot," Celestine announced, taking her coat and the new scarf.

"I was afraid of that," he muttered, leaving the store.

Celestine said good-bye to Emily and thanked her for the scarves. Then she ran to the train depot. The news that the train was late stopped on the tracks somewhere and possibly attacked by robbers had spread all over town. The waiting room at the depot was warm, heated by a pot-bellied stove, but Celestine was too anxious to wait inside. She ran outside every so often looking along the tracks.

"Miss Tillman, I didn't think I'd see you here." She heard a voice she dreaded hearing again.

She'd learned a long time ago that it was not good to avoid confrontations. They had a way of finding you. Perhaps under less stressful circumstances, she might have answered politely and walked in the opposite direction. Or maybe not. She hated bullies and Mrs.

Miller was one of the worst. "Why not, Mrs. Miller? It's a free country. People come and go as they please."

Mrs. Miller shook her finger at her. "Don't be cheeky, girl. I thought you'd not dare show your face in town after insulting one of the most important ladies here, Mrs. Cora Lynn Turner."

"Mrs. Turner shouldn't slap the seamstress and should pay for her orders if she wants to be treated with respect."

"Her behavior is always faultless, while you've caused a lot of trouble in the short time since you've arrived in town. You live in a house full of bachelors…"

"I live alone in the house. All the bachelors live in the bunkhouse," Celestine corrected her.

Mrs. Miller was on a row and paid her no attention. "You insulted Mrs. Turner at the dressmaker in full view of the onlookers, creating a public scandal. Your outrageous behavior continued by engaging into a fight with disreputable men in front of the saloon, no less. One wonders what will happen next?"

"A fight at the train depot with you, I suppose.

And you'll claim that I started it, no doubt." Celestine looked again at the tracks. Was that a steam from the engine in the distance? No, it was just a puffy cloud. "Although I'm kind of busy right now. But I'll be in church tomorrow if you want to continue our talk."

Mrs. Miller opened her mouth to express her outrage, but the young man working at the depot came running. "Miss Tillman, rancher Richardson arrived with news."

Forgetting Mrs. Miller, Celestine ran after him. She found the rancher behind the depot talking with the master.

"A handcar and six people should be adequate. They were not large rocks, but could derail a train at high speed," Richardson explained.

"Mr. Richardson, is Mr. Maitland all right?" Celestine asked anxiously.

"Yes, Miss Tillman, he's fine. The robbers have been caught and the sheriff is guarding them. Maitland found his brother and he should be arriving any minute now." He smiled.

He was a handsome devil. No wonder Emily sighed every time he passed in the street outside her window, Celestine thought.

The depot master quickly assembled a crew. Four in the handcar and two volunteers on horses departed immediately to clear the tracks for the stranded train. Then he explained to the crowd of anxious people gathered there that the gang of robbers, probably 'Flat Nose' George, had been apprehended almost in the entirety and the train will arrive in half an hour max at the station. Nobody was injured and the valuables had been recovered.

It was another twenty minutes before Celestine saw a slow-moving horse coming along the tracks. Impatient, and to warm up her frozen feet, she stomped her feet in the snow. Was it Elliott?

When the horse came closer, she saw it was burdened with two people and two large packages. No wonder it was walking so slowly. One of the people was Elliott, and Celestine felt all the fear drain out of her. He was alive and well. She ran to him without thinking, skirts flying.

Elliott vaulted down and handed the package to the man in the saddle. Then he opened his arms wide to catch her.

"I was so worried when the young man told me that you went with the sheriff to catch the robbers," she said, her face burrowed in his plaid shirt and holding him around the middle.

It never occurred to Elliott that someone could be worried for him. It was a new feeling. Nobody ever worried or gave him another thought in his life. Maybe his mother had loved him as Orville wrote in his letter, but certainly she never expressed any worry or feelings for him. It made him warm and fuzzy to think that he mattered so much to one special person.

"I didn't know you were married, brother." The second man dismounted, careful with his burden, who shook, sneezed, and a little girl with red curls, came out of the blanket, looking at Celestine with curiosity.

Elliott turned to his brother. "I'm not married. This is Miss Celestine Tillman who is staying with me for the moment."

"I'm the new teacher in town," she supplied the explanation looking at him. Orville Maitland was very different than his brother. He was an inch shorter and while Elliott was dark and brooding, Orville had a light-brown hair and blue eyes, twinkling benevolently from under his round glasses. In fact, Celestine could hardly see any resemblance or family traits.

"Teacher, hmm? This is my daughter, Annabelle."

"I'm glad you arrived just in time to celebrate Christmas with us."

"Do you have a Christmas tree?" Annabelle asked with the directness of children. "Papa said that we'll have a big tree at the hotel."

"I don't know about that, but I assure you that ours is grand, with all sorts of decorations. We're going home soon and you'll see," Celestine assured her.

This stopped the men, Elliott untying Orville's portmanteau from the horse and Orville trying to pick it up while holding Annabelle with the other hand.

"We have a room at the hotel," Orville said.

"Where are they going to sleep?" Elliott asked, more practical.

"Annabelle can sleep with me in the big bedroom. The bed is big enough for two and you two can sleep in the loft if there is no room in the bunkhouse."

Elliott looked at Celestine's stubborn face and knew it had been decided. He didn't know how he felt about sharing a loft with his brother with whom he had never shared anything. It was weird.

He pulled the horse's bridle to return it to the depot master.

CHAPTER 16

With a shrill whistle, the train entered in the depot to the cheers of all present there. Weary passengers descended to be met by relatives or just to warm up in the depot's waiting room and to get their valuables from the sheriff.

Orville and Elliott, already warmed up, went to recover the trunk from the freight car and to load it in the wagon. Annabelle was holding Celestine's hand and asking a lot of questions about the ranch and the Christmas celebration.

Finally, they were on their way to the ranch. Elliott was driving the wagon, with Celestine near him on the seat. Orville was in the wagon with Annabelle bundled up in blankets propped against the trunk.

"Interesting country here and so different from the east," Orville remarked, looking around at the vast white open plains around them.

They had a lot of things to talk about and the landscape was not among them, but now was not the time. They needed privacy. Elliott turned to answer him, when he saw four riders galloping at high speed to catch up with them. They were still at a distance, but approaching fast. If he was not mistaken, the pinto horse in front belonged to Crawford. It would be impossible to outrun them with the wagon.

"Crawford," he told Celestine and transferred the reins to her. He grabbed the Winchester rifle at his feet and checked it for readiness. Celestine took a Colt out of her reticule and placed it on her lap, while holding the reins with one hand. "I'm sorry, brother. You've landed in the middle of a range war. One of the ranchers wants to chase us from our land."

"Well, robbers and greedy neighbors are everywhere. Maybe not overt in their intentions, but just as ruthless," Orville commented. "I'm not helpless or I wouldn't have started this journey west." He looked at the approaching riders.

"There is another loaded rifle at the bottom of the wagon."

Celestine half turned to look back and to talk to

him. "My father used to say, when you are attacked by a gang and have only one chance, hit the leader. The rest of them will be confused and will disband."

"Good idea, Celestine," Elliott agreed. "Orville, are you as good a shooter as you were in our youth? Aim above the head of the leader who's riding the pinto horse. I'll shoot between the front legs of the horse. Wait until I say, 'now'."

Celestine could have told him also that life didn't always happened as we planned, but there was no more time and the riders were upon them.

"Maitland, how fortuitous to find you," Crawford said from atop his nervously prancing and snorting horse.

"Yes, indeed," Elliott answered in kind. "I just caught a gang of train robbers. I was wondering with what I should crown my day." He stretched his leg to the side and raised his rifle.

This took Crawford aback, but not for long. "You know you have no chance. If Miller signs his ranch over to me, then you are next. Parker is too far away to help you."

"This is my home and ranching is my life. I'm not selling, not ever. Is this clear enough for you?" Elliott answered.

Crawford straightened in the saddle. "You'll regret it. I've decided that with every passing day my offer will go down and become lower. It's your money to lose."

Elliott scoffed. "Your offer was pitiful the way it was. But money is not the issue here. You can offer me ten times the value of my land and my answer will remain the same. I'm not selling."

"You will. When your cattle drop dead like Miller's prize bull, you'll have no choice," Crawford argued with arrogance. "I see you brought people to help you. First, the schoolteacher. She's not much to look at…"

Celestine smiled. "Maybe not, but I'm notorious in town. And I beat away three of your men."

Technically, it was true, so Crawford coughed. "With that toy gun of yours?"

"With whatever I have handy." Lifting one hand

to her tattered hat with cherries, she extracted a long hat pin. "It's poisoned and lethal," she joked. By the horrified looks exchanged by Crawford's men, they thought she meant it.

"What about the man in the wagon?" Crawford asked, pointing at Orville, who, with his round glasses and placid face looked more like a timid teacher than a hardened ranch hand.

"And what do we have here?" One of the Crawford's men came closer and leaned down to look in the wagon.

Annabelle, who had waited patiently under her blankets until then, raised her arm and hit him in the face with a rock. The man howled in pain and went for his gun only to have it blown off his hand by Orville.

Elliott stood up, rifle in hand. "Nobody move."

Celestine saw another man, his hand inching closer to his holster to pull out his gun. "Watch out, Elliott."

Elliott pointed his rifle at the man. "Do it and you lose your hand." It was time to end this cat and mouse game. Eyeing the nervous pinto that Crawford made efforts to restrain, Elliott said, "Now" and shot somewhere in front of the horse. In the same moment, Orville aimed and fired. Crawford's hat flew from his head.

It was too much for the nervous animal. He rose on his hind legs almost unseating Crawford, then stepped back and ran away with his rider barely holding in the saddle. Exactly as Celestine had predicted, the other three men looked at each other, then at the two rifles pointed at them, and decided to follow their boss.

"You'll hear from us," one of them threatened before riding away after the others.

"Yeah, I guess I will," Elliott muttered and placed his rifle at his feet. "I'm sorry Orville. Maybe it was a bad idea to bring you here."

"Why? It was invigorating. I'm not leaving until this situation with Crawford gets solved."

"It might never be…"

"Oh, it will be. I know the likes of Crawford. He's not a patient man. He wants the land and he wants it now. He'll make his move soon," Orville said.

"And we'll fight and kill the bad man," Annabelle piped from under her blankets.

Orville seemed to hesitate for the first time. "Maybe Annabelle would be safer at the hotel."

"Nonsense," Celestine argued. "Women and children have been present when a fort was under assault and they did their share. But, for your peace of mind, I'll take care of her, and make sure to keep her in a safe place."

Orville nodded. "All right. Now, tell me about your neighbors."

Elliott started the wagon. "Crawford wants my ranch because it's closer to town and convenient to the secondary country road. Farther from me, beyond the cursed Dargill Creek, is John Parker's land. He is a good friend and he'll never sell. He's my age and ready to fight. Between me and Crawford is Emory Miller's land. He has seven children, but the two oldest boys have gone panning for gold in Colorado and are not interested in the ranch. The next two are girls. They are fluff heads like their mother, interested only in gossip. The last three are too young. If you add to this that Miller owes the bank a lot of money for buying his prize bull, you'll see he is in a tight situation and he might take Crawford's offer."

"I see. What about the fellow who was with you in the train?"

"Lloyd Richardson. He has a large ranch, more to the northeast from here and somewhat isolated, in a remote area. Crawford wants his land because it borders his to the west and because it has a nice creek, a good source of water for the cattle. Also there is a deep canyon behind his house and people are saying that there might be gold there. Richardson swears there isn't and most believe him. He'd be richer if he had gold on his land. But I guess Crawford thinks there is."

"Why did he build his house so close to the canyon?"

"Because it's the highest point and he can see the whole valley bellow. It's a nice place for a house. There is another piece of land farther north from him. It's unclear what happened to the owner. It is abandoned now, and Crawford tried but couldn't buy it."

The ranch house in the distance was a welcome sight. Carried by the monotonous trot of the horses, Annabelle had fallen asleep, after all the adventures she'd been through. When the wagon stopped in front of the house, she perked up as soon as she heard the little dog barking.

The dog was waiting at the door, agitated now that he felt Celestine was back. When he saw Annabelle, he plopped down and inclined his head to study the newcomer.

"Let him sniff your hand, to get to know you," Celestine told the little girl.

Annabelle extended her hand and the puppy came closer cautiously, sniffed her hand, then satisfied, he gave her a doggy grin, and wagged his tail like saying, let's play. Soon after, the girl and the dog were running around the room.

When Annabelle saw the decorated Christmas tree she clapped her hands happily declaring, just like the ranch hands had before, that it was the most beautiful tree she'd ever seen in her four years of life.

"I don't know where she gets such energy," Orville commented, sitting wearily on a chair at the kitchen table. The stew that Celestine had left to simmer on the stove all day smelled appetizing and his stomach growled.

Soon the kitchen filled with ranch hands and Celestine ladled the rich stew in bowls. It was funny to see the rough cowboys looking in wonder at the little girl with red curly hair dressed in boy's clothes, which was easier on the road, Orville explained.

When their hunger was appeased, they had coffee and peach cobbler for desert.

Frank looked at Celestine, then at the little girl playing in front of the tree with the dog. He leaned forward and said in a low voice. "We found a calf killed close to Dargill Creek. What's weird is the way it was killed with one of those Indian arrows you saw the other week."

A calf was a loss he couldn't afford, Elliott thought. "Four Fingers, what do you think?"

The Indian kept silent for a long time. "The arrow is not Indian. It's made for show. I think there is a man camping there at Dargill Creek or in the caves below. He is hiding and is not from here."

"An outlaw?"

"Possibly."

"I'll go tomorrow to investigate," Elliott said.

"Tomorrow is Christmas and we are all going to church. There will be presents under the tree for everybody and a good festive meal on the table," Celestine announced.

CHAPTER 17

The house was quiet. Only an occasional crackle from the wood in the fireplace interrupted the silence. The heat rose and the loft was warm and cozy. Elliott was glad they had chosen the loft to sleep and not the second smaller bedroom that was drafty and cold. There was no noise from Celestine and Annabelle's bedroom, a sign that the girl had fallen asleep as soon as her head had hit the pillow. They were all tired after this day full of events. Orville had been quiet for awhile. Maybe he was asleep. Elliott had no idea if his brother snored or not.

As if guessing his thoughts, Orville chuckled. "I am tired to the bones and yet I'm wide awake."

"New place, new people."

"These last few days, I've slept in trains, waiting rooms, and dingy hotel rooms. This loft is very pleasant." He sighed. "All day, I wished we had privacy to talk, and now that we do, I find it awkward."

"Perhaps because we have grown up like

strangers, living in the same house, but in two different worlds, " Elliott observed, looking at the logs from the ceiling in the dim light provided by the fireplace downstairs.

"Yes, we have to talk about that too. But first, I want to thank you for the heroic way you saved the train from the robbers."

Elliott shrugged. "This is our life here on the frontier, in Wyoming Territory. There are outlaws and robbers. We do our best to protect lives and goods from them. The train is our lifeline and we want to keep it as safe as possible, or the Union Pacific Company could abandon the line if they have big losses."

"I understand. Nevertheless, I am thankful. You have no idea what terror I felt when I raised my eyes from the book and I saw that Annabelle was not with me. I wanted to go search for her, but the robber at the end of the car, shot in my direction. I figured a bad parent was better than a dead one. Where did you find her?"

Elliott pondered if he should tell him the truth. As a father, Orville had the right to know. "In the last car.

One of the robbers had taken her hostage. When she saw me, she bit him on the hand. I don't think she was frightened."

"No, she's fearless. I thought she'd complain that we left home for an uncertain future, but she never did. She looks forward to every day to explore and discover new things. What else did she do?"

"Nothing, we brought her straight to you... Except that on the way, she proposed to Lloyd Richardson."

"Proposed what?"

"To marry him when she'll grow up."

Orville rubbed his eyes. "What am I going to do with her?"

"Keep up. You have no choice. With her red curls and dainty figure, she resembles Joanna, but her mother was more subdued, even shy. She's a whirlwind."

"Papa didn't even want to look at her. In his mind, only a boy was important to continue his apothecary dynasty. In the end, nobody did. I sold each and every store separately and decided to live an entirely different life away from Virginia."

"He certainly didn't want me to get involved...."
Elliott remembered how he had been rejected by his
father. "You were the heir and I didn't matter. In fact, he
raised us separately. We never played together like
brothers do."

"I have an idea why, but I have no proof. I
wanted to talk to you. As I wrote to you, Mama was very
distressed after you left."

"She never showed distress when our father
unjustly berated me or when he beat the tar out of me
with his belt," Elliott remarked bitterly.

"I think she couldn't, even if she wanted. I think
she had an understanding with Papa." Orville halted a
moment before saying, "I think Papa was not your
father."

"What?" Elliott asked loudly, then again in a
lower voice, "What did you say?"

"I don't have any proof, but when Mama fell ill,
she waited for a moment when Papa was not nearby, and
she pressed in my hand two things, a garnet ring she

wore on a chain at her neck and a picture of a cavalry man on top of a horse. 'For Elliott,' she whispered. I have them with me and I'll give them to you tomorrow."

Elliott lit a gas lamp and looked at Orville. "You don't throw such news at me and expect me to sleep in peace. Please, show me the picture and tell me what you know."

"Shh! You'll wake up the girls. I told you, it's just my feeling, thinking about our childhood and family life. Yes, you are right. Papa was grossly unfair to you most of the time. He kept us separate from the time we were kids. Mama never interfered because she was afraid Papa would reveal to the world that you were not his son. That's what I think. She was wrong. Papa was too proud to admit such a thing to the world. Or maybe she knew, but didn't want to risk his wrath by taking your side. After you left, it was like she had nothing more to lose."

Orville made his way downstairs and extracted from his portmanteau a thick package. He climbed back to the loft and handed Elliott the package.

"It's almost midnight. Merry Christmas, brother. I

don't know if this is good or bad news for you, but you are entitled to know the truth."

Elliott opened the package and he found inside a garnet ring on a gold chain, a picture of a dashing officer on a horse, and a thick leather bound book. He studied the picture framed in a simple thin silver frame. "I remember that Mama took me to the train station and I was maybe four years old and very scared of the huge black monsters belching smoke, the locomotives. Mama was crying and introduced me to a dashing officer. Unfortunately, I don't remember him well. It's all fuzzy like in a dream."

"I don't think it was a dream," Orville said gently.

Elliott looked at the picture in his hand and then at the book. "Hey, this is our family bible. Why did you give it to me?"

"Because Mama gave me all these three things together. At the time, I thought that it was because Papa had just entered the room. But then I decided to bring them all to you as Mama gave them to me. I thought there might be some letter or explanation inside, but I found nothing."

Elliott leafed through it and indeed there was no hidden paper inside. "I guess I'll never know who my father is. Look at me, I'm a mature man, with a ranch and a life of my own and I have no idea where I come from. I have only a picture – and I thank you for it – but no name. The bible has nothing written inside except the Maitland family members, when they were born and when they died." He looked inside at the different penmanship. "A lot of Elliott-s in the family tree. If I didn't belong there, I wonder why Mama named me Elliott. To appease Papa probably."

Orville frowned. "Let me see. Grandpa was named Elliott." He bent to look over Elliott's shoulder. "He had three sons. William, the eldest, Papa James was the second and Elliott, the third. William had only one son, named Elliott and two girls. Strange." He pointed at the old writing. "This Elliott, our uncle, died at thirty-six."

"Why do you suppose his name is crossed out

with ink?"

"I remember words whispered in the kitchen when I was a little boy, that Uncle Elliott was a major in the Union Army. He died in the last days of the war, but the family never forgave him. Wait! I remember the cook telling Elise that he died and poor Mama can't even mourn him properly."

They looked at each other.

"This might be it. The family secret. Look at his name, Elliott Robert Maitland. Just like yours," Orville said.

Elliott kept silent for a long time. He closed the bible slowly and placed the picture on top of it. "You're probably right. So I am a Maitland after all. Of course, I had no father. The one who raised me, resented me and punished me at every turn, and the other one, carelessly conceived me, and then left to pursue his military career and to get himself killed. Neither one cared about me. And Mama was too frightened to care."

"But you have a brother. I hope you'll accept me as such, if it's not too late to mend our connection. I would like that very much. Not because Mama said so. I did what she asked of me. You are my closest relative left. I don't know what life I'll have in California, but I'd like to believe that here in Wyoming I have a brother who's thinking of me." Orville extended his hand.

"I'd like that too," Elliott shook his hand and for the first time the two Maitland brothers hugged each other.

"Now, let's sleep. It will be morning soon." Elliott turned off the gas lamp.

In the dark, Orville said, "There is one more thing you need to know. I have always envied you for the freedom of being yourself and not the heir to the apothecary business."

"Seriously? I thought you were happy to be…"

"Nope. I even hated entering an apothecary shop. The medicinal smell made me nauseous."

"It's Christmas Day!" Annabelle announced gleefully and ran into the living room to the Christmas tree, the little dog at her heels, barking to be included in the fun play.

Upstairs in the loft, Orville placed his arm over his eyes. "Is it morning yet?"

"Almost. But I hear chirping downstairs, so we'd better get dressed," Elliott answered, smiling.

"There are lots and lots of gifts under the tree. Santa Claus came earlier. Can I open them, Celestine?" Annabelle's voice piped from the living room.

Celestine was at the stove preparing biscuits and flapjacks and fluffy eggs with bacon for breakfast before going to church. "Only the ones with your name on them, Annabelle." She wanted to say that the opening of the gifts should be done with everyone present in the room, after coming back from town. Then she remembered from her childhood the excitement of finding treasured gifts under the tree and her impatience to see what's inside the carefully wrapped packages.

Annabelle had already torn into the paper of the larger box. "A doll," she cried happily. "Can I call her Dolly?"

Upstairs, Orville paused buttoning his vest over

his good white shirt. "A doll? I didn't buy her a doll."

Elliott looked at him sheepishly. "I did. I mean, Celestine claimed that a doll is a must for a little girl."

Orville felt his eyes moisten with emotion. "I don't know what exactly you are waiting for, but Celestine is a treasure of a woman. You'd better hurry up and stake your claim before another man does."

Elliott stiffened. "Do you want her?"

"Want her? What are you talking about? I'm a married man," Orville protested. Then, realizing what he'd said, he covered his mouth with his hand.

"I'm sorry, Orville," Elliott said, patting him on the back.

Orville's face crumpled. "I want my Joanna, the only woman I've ever wanted. Why was she taken from me?" He shook his head. "It's not fair."

"Papa, come to see my doll," Annabelle shouted from downstairs.

"Well, you have no time for self-pity. You have a daughter like no other to keep you on your toes," Elliott told him, descending down the ladder.

CHAPTER 18

Orville helped Annabelle open another large package that contained a blue velvet dress, complete with white socks, shoes, and a blue bonnet.

Smiling, Celestine straightened the girl's blue bow from her hair and walked into the parlor to take another wrapped small package from her trunk. When she turned, she saw that Elliott had followed her.

"Celestine, this is for you, Merry Christmas," he said, giving her a long navy blue coat, made of soft wool. "You can't spend winter in Wyoming wrapped in a blanket. You need a thick coat and gloves," he added, placing the coat on her shoulders.

Celestine knew that according to the rules of good deportment, a woman shouldn't accept pieces of clothing from a man who was not a close relative. But rules be darned, the coat was beautiful and warm and she needed it. She was a practical woman and this was not exactly Philadelphia society with their rigid rules. She buried her face in the softness of the fabric. "Thank you,

Elliott. I've never had such a beautiful coat. Where did you find it? I don't think Sam carried this at the mercantile."

Breathing easier now that she'd accepted his gift, Elliott smiled. "I bought it at Trabing. They carry high quality merchandise. I hope you like it."

"I love it. I know you shouldn't give me this and I shouldn't accept it. Mrs. Miller would have many things to say if she knew, but thank you, I love it and I needed it. You're a wonderful man." She handed him her small package. "This is for you."

Elliott opened the wrap and the box and found inside a pocket watch on a gold chain.

"It belonged to my father," Celestine said biting her lower lip. Maybe he already had a watch or maybe he didn't like it.

Realizing how much it meant to her, Elliott felt his heart warming. No one had ever thought to give him a gift beyond practical, socks, shoes, gloves, not even candies were allowed to have for Christmas. The boys would get spoiled, their father claimed. "Celestine, this is too precious to you. You need to be able to remember your father…"

"The memories of him are here," she touched her forehead. "I'll remember him always, his kind smile, the way he narrowed his eyes when he read an important paper – I think he needed glasses – his special wink to tell me that we are together in life. I don't need the watch to remember him. I can't think of a better person to have it. You took me into your house and gave me shelter when I was scared, lost in a strange town, where no one waited for me at the train depot. You are a good man, Elliott." She rose on her toes and kissed his cheek.

Elliott circled her waist as he had many times, helping her up and down from the wagon seat. He pulled her closer. Her golden eyes were bright with emotion. How had she become so precious to him in such a short time? He touched his lips to hers. She didn't step back. She kept looking at him in the semi-darkness of the parlor, waiting for more from him. Untutored, yet curious of this entirely new feeling of warmth. He pulled her closer and deepened the kiss.

Annabelle's squeal of delight from the other room and men's voices made him regretfully step back.

There were little gifts for everyone. Peppermints and licorice in every package, and bonus money from Elliott to each of his men.

Annabelle was hugging to her chest a crudely whittled dog from Four Fingers that bore some resemblance to the little dog that was lying on the rug in front of the fireplace, tired of so much excitement.

Joe opened the package with his name on it and found an illustrated copy of Fenimore Cooper's "The Last of the Mohicans". He looked at it and bent his head. Baffled by his reaction, Celestine said, "It's a good adventure book. I read it many times when I was a teenager."

It was the Pirate who wiped the syrup off his curled mustache and answered her. "The book is wasted on Joe. He doesn't know how to read."

Celestine looked at Joe, surprised. Red faced with embarrassment, he nodded. "It's true. My brother and I grew up in an orphanage. Nobody bothered to teach us anything. We've worked since we were eight."

"I can teach you if you want. I'm a teacher."

Joe looked at Celestine with doubt. Annabelle grabbed his hand. "We could learn together, Joe. I know a few letters, but I want to know them all and to read all the books Papa has. Wouldn't that be wonderful?" she asked jumping up and down.

"Yeah," Joe agreed with half voice.

They bundled up to go to church. Celestine looked lovely in her new navy blue coat.

"In all my five years of ranching here, I haven't been to town as often as in these past few days," Elliott grumbled, secretly admiring the way the new coat showed off Celestine's natural elegant posture and graceful walk.

Celestine entered the church holding Annabelle's hand. She saw Emily Parker in the back row. "Come sit with us," she mouthed, but Emily smiled sadly and waved her on. Advancing, she heard some ladies talking.

"She has a child?"

"The girl doesn't look like Maitland or like the other gentleman."

Celestine smiled. How absurd were these gossipy women. She took a seat in the third pew from the front, with Elliott and Orville at her side and the little girl near her. The service reminded Celestine of the happy times when she'd celebrated Christmas with her father. Singing together with the rest of the congregation brought tears to her eyes.

At the end of the service, Celestine looked for Emily, but she couldn't see her. Probably she'd left early. She saw Lloyd Richardson with a beautiful woman, but pale and sad.

"Is that his wife?" she asked Elliott.

"No, that's his sister, Esmé. She doesn't come into town often. She's weird," he explained, dismissing the subject.

Prudence Parker came closer and hugged Celestine. She offered Annabelle a small stuffed bear. "Don't ask who gave me this. My boys are past playing with such toys."

Annabelle beamed at her, showing two adorable dimples in her cheeks. "Thank you."

After talking to the men, the sheriff pulled off his hat and saluted Celestine. "Miss Tillman, Maitland explained to me that you prepared a scrumptious meal and you are all going home for a Christmas feast, but I have a few things to talk to him about."

Celestine shook her finger at him. "No more chasing train robbers or other adventures, leaving me behind."

"No, ma'am. No more adventures without you," the sheriff assured her, his moustache twitching with laughter.

"We can take them home, Maitland," Prudence interfered, linking her arm with Celestine. "And we'll wait until you return."

Elliott exchanged a glance with John Parker and nodded. Only Orville seemed unconvinced, worried to be parted from Annabelle.

"Orville, I'll take good care of her, I swear," Celestine promised.

"Yes, Papa. I'll go with Celestine," Annabelle confirmed, jumping from one foot to the other. The frozen snow crunched under her small feet.

"I think the young lady needs to be wrapped in blankets," Parker said bringing his buggy closer.

Celestine turned to the sheriff before climbing in. "I don't know you well, but if you are alone and have nothing planned, Sheriff, please come to have Christmas meal with us."

"I'm a bachelor. It's kind of you, thank you," The sheriff didn't mention that he planned to spend his evening with Dora, one of the girls from the saloon. He was not a man with vices, but from time to time a man like him was bound to feel lonely. "It might be best if I stayed in town just in case I'm needed."

After Parker's buggy departed, Elliott and Orville followed the sheriff to his office. "Nice woman, Miss Tillman," the sheriff said, unlocking the door to his office. "And I heard she's a great cook. It won't be long and a lucky man will take her off your hands, Maitland."

"Not if they want to live," Elliott muttered

clenching his fists.

"I didn't hear you," the sheriff lifted the blue enameled coffee pot from the top of the pot-bellied stove. "Coffee is all I have. But it's hot and it's good in this cold weather." He poured coffee in three tin cups and handed them to the brothers.

"So, I wanted to ask you Mr. Maitland what valuables have the train robbers stolen from you."

"Not much. Annabelle's locket, but Elliott returned it to us."

"A locket?" The sheriff looked at Elliott, raising his eyebrow in question.

"One of the robbers dropped it when we fought on the car roof. I forgot about it until Orville told me about the girl's locket. The reason I returned it to her without checking with you, was that I was sure it was hers. You see, I knew Joanna, the girl's mother, all my life. She was our neighbor's daughter. Her picture was inside the locket," Elliott explained.

"Ah, all right then. What happened to the girl's mother, if you don't mind my asking?"

"She died in childbirth three months ago. I decided I had to change my life or I'd go crazy," Orville told him and his voice shook with emotion. "Sorry. I'm still raw."

"I understand. In fact, all the people going west hide secrets or had tragedies in their previous lives. They come west to build a new life and forget the old hurt." The sheriff added, sipping his hot coffee slowly. "Do you intend to stay here?"

Orville shrugged. "Joanna and I used to dream of going to California. But for now, I'm staying to help Elliott until I'm sure no one is threatening him."

"There are always opportunities here. I'm looking for a good deputy myself." The sheriff looked Orville up and down. "Or maybe that's not your cup of tea."

Elliott laughed. "Orville's calm demeanor and his glasses make people think he's a pushover. He's one of the fastest men with a gun and his aim is right on target, glasses and all."

"Really?" The sheriff rose and threw Orville a holster. Reluctantly, Orville belted it around his hips.

"When I say three," the sheriff said. "One, two..."

When he said three, he had his hand on the gun, while Orville pointed it at him.

"Well, I'll be darned. You are good. Maybe you would consider that deputy job. It doesn't pay much and you have to run all over the county after outlaws."

"Very tempting," Orville commented dryly, returning the gun and the holster to the sheriff.

CHAPTER 19

"Did the robbers take any other valuables from you?" the sheriff asked Orville.

"Only a few dollars and some change in a fancy pouch. I threw it at their feet and they grabbed it without looking inside. I had no jewelry or watch on my person. Most of my money was well hidden."

"Hmm, I found no fancy pouch on the robbers we apprehended."

"No problem. It was not much."

The sheriff leaned back in his chair. "One of the robbers escaped." He pulled out several Wanted posters. "Do you recognize any one from these Wanted men?"

The pictures were not clear. Elliott was ready to go home, when one of them struck a memory. A youthful head looking up, asking, 'Are you still there, Zeb?' He looked again at the poster. "This one. Without a doubt. The picture is grainy, but he is the one that escaped. The look, the glint in the eye."

The sheriff nodded satisfied. "Good. Thank you."

The door opened, bringing in a wave of frosty air and the owner of one of the saloons, Tom Wilkes. He was not as calm as usual or as full of self-importance. In fact, he was rather disturbed. "Sheriff, you have to come quickly. The banker Turner came in threatening me and asking me to tell him where his wife was. He almost destroyed everything in his path from room to room upstairs and serious patrons and respectable people in town had to run away in various state of undress. The crazy man was firing a gun all over the place. It seems he knew his wife was gambling, but finding her in her petticoats didn't improve his mood."

The sheriff grabbed his holster, threw another at Orville and ran out. "The idiot shouldn't have married a woman thirty years younger than him."

"He shouldn't have married Cora Lynn, period," the saloon owner said, breathing hard. "My girls have more sense of propriety than she has."

It was like a tornado had gone through the saloon. Tables turned upside down, chairs with broken legs. Broken bottles and playing cards on the floor, draperies torn. Everything reeked of cheap whisky. A few men were throwing punches at each other, but without much enthusiasm because they were more interested in the drama going on upstairs. The sheriff grabbed two of the most avid punchers by the scruff of their neck and threw them out the door. Elliott and Orville were ready to intervene, but the fight died down. Even the piano player who had continued to play a lively tune throughout the entire fracas, now stopped and looked at the sheriff.

"Did the banker do all this?" the sheriff asked.

"You know how it is. The banker came in yelling and started to push his way around and it was the spark that started the fire. In no time at all, the men started to punch each other. Now what shall I do?" the saloon owner asked distressed, looking at the painting of a naked woman over the bar that sported a fresh bullet hole.

"Make a list of all the damages. The banker is good to pay."

A woman's shrill voice yelling hysterically upstairs was mixed with an angry male baritone. From time to time, the voices were covered by the noise of an object thrown to the floor.

The sheriff looked up. "I'm going upstairs. Maitland, could you keep an eye on things here. I doubt the fighting will start again, but just in case. Orville come with me, please."

"Sheriff, be careful. The banker has a gun and he's shooting all over the place. He's not a dangerous criminal, but he's in a bad mood," the saloon owner said.

The sheriff stopped in front of the door where the yelling could be heard, and pushed it opened with his foot, then stepped aside. A shot came through.

"Hands up, Turner. Stop the heroics before anyone gets hurt." He advanced in the doorway cautiously, then dived for the gun wavering wildly in the banker's hand. Orville positioned himself behind the sheriff, with his gun drawn. But the fight had gone out of the elderly banker. He collapsed in the only chair still standing in the room.

"How could the woman I married do this to me? She gambled away my money and cuckolded me with

Miller's foreman."

The sheriff checked the gun and emptied the chamber, then returned it to the banker. "I'm a bachelor, Turner, and there is a good reason why I prefer it this way. Now let's go downstairs where you'll pay Tom Wilkes for the damages you caused to his establishment."

This got him out of his stupor. "I'm not paying anything. It's his fault for having a saloon where people gamble," the banker protested vehemently.

"Oh yes, you'll pay. Otherwise, you'll spend the night in jail for disturbing the peace in town on this sacred day of Christmas and destroying one of the businesses." The sheriff grabbed the banker's arm and pulled him up.

This propelled Cora Lynn forward. "What about my dress? It has a hundred tiny buttons. Perhaps you could help me, Sheriff," she said fluttering her eyelashes at him.

"Not me, ma'am. I figure, if you succeeded to take it off, you'll put it on just as easily. If not, I'm sure Tom will lend you these red draperies to wrap yourself in. Now let's go."

It was quite late when the two Maitland brothers went to the stable where the wagon was and left the town behind.

"The good news is that if Crawford was waiting for me, then he was transformed into an icicle by now. But I sure am glad that I'm not alone and that I have you with me. Merry Christmas, Orville."

Orville smiled. "Merry Christmas to you, too. I promise I'll stay until you are safe from this Crawford." They drove the wagon in companionable silence for a while until Orville started talking again. "It's so different here than in Virginia. It's such a wide open space, wild and untouched by man. Are you happy here, Elliott?"

"I had to work hard to make this ranch profitable and to learn how to be a rancher. Am I happy? Is anybody truly happy? I don't know. What I know without a doubt is that this is my land and my home and I'd give my life to protect it. This is where I belong and I couldn't live anywhere else."

"Good for you. I don't know where my place on

this earth is. I still have to find it. I don't think I can be happy, not without Joanna, but I want to find a place where I'll be at peace."

At the ranch house, Celestine assured the Parkers she'd be fine and urged them to go home and enjoy the Christmas dinner with their family. She wanted to ask Prudence some questions about Emily and what caused the rift between her and the Parkers, but now was not the moment, not with her husband present.

The Parkers left and Celestine arranged a festive table with china she found in the parlor instead of tin plates. From time to time, she ran to the window to look outside, but the snowy white landscape was unperturbed and there was no sign of Elliott.

Annabelle, after playing with the dog under the Christmas tree, had fallen asleep on the rug in front of the fireplace.

After three long hours, when Celestine had worn a path to the window and was ready to send one of the men to town to see what happened, she heard noise outside. She opened the door and walked out on the porch. It was cold, but Celestine didn't feel it. She had eyes only for the approaching wagon.

When the wagon stopped in front of the barn she ran to it. "What took you so long? Do you know how worried I've been? I was ready to send the men after you." She realized she was acting like a shrew, but her pent-up fear had to be released.

Elliott vaulted down. Laughing, he grabbed her waist and twirled her around. "You won't believe what happened in town. But first, how about we eat that food you've been preparing for days."

The men were hungry and they gathered around the table. At first, they were slightly intimidated by the crisp white tablecloth and delicate porcelain plates, but the platters with roast beef and potatoes, pork rolls, a special recipe from Celestine's old cook, and chicken in sour cream sauce made their mouth water.

For desert, Celestine had made them apple pie as promised and an Austrian cake that was popular in the east, Linzer torte. At the end, she filled their cups with hot coffee. Then they sang carols and Celestine read Christmas stories from a thick book.

Later, much later into the night, the ranch hands went to the bunkhouse and the house was quiet. Only the stone fireplace provided heat and made the few glass ornaments in the tree glow with a magic light. The man who lingered in the room after every one left was not looking at the tree. Standing near the window, he was searching the dark sky for a bright star.

"Merry Christmas, Joanna, wherever you are up there in heaven, in a much better world. Our first Christmas without you. We missed you so much. I hope you can see our daughter growing. Sometimes I wonder how could two ordinary people like us create such a bright spirit, beautiful, smart and fearless like Annabelle… I know we planned to go to California together and I wanted to fulfill your dream, but for the moment I think I'll stay here. Elliott needs me and I discovered that I need him. Help me find my place, Joanna. I'm lost without you."

He touched his lips with his fingers and then

placed his hand on the icy glass looking at the bright star up in the dark sky.

CHAPTER 20

"Well Orville, you might not be a rancher, but Annabelle was born in the saddle," Elliott said next morning after Christmas, looking at his tiny niece, whose happy cries filled the yard.

Four Fingers had brought an old, placid mare out of the barn and he placed Annabelle in the saddle. Then leading the horse by the bridle, he pulled her around the corral. Not only was the little girl not scared by the large animal, but also she banged her feet to the mare's flanks, prodding her, "Faster, horsey, faster."

In the kitchen, Celestine was washing the last of the breakfast dishes and thinking that now with Christmas over, she only had another week until New Year and then she'd have to move to town. She would have to live either in the teacher's quarters or if that job didn't work out, then she'd have to look for another job.

Frank refreshed his coffee and stopped to look at the Christmas tree. "It sure was a pretty tree, Miss Celestine. I'm sorry to see it go. It brought a little beauty and joy into our lives."

"We'll keep it until after the New Year and next year we'll make an even better one," Celestine assured him.

Outside, Joe returned riding quickly. He dismounted and went to talk to Elliott. "I went to fix the fence with Parker and detoured farther north to look at the cattle. There was another animal killed with an arrow."

"Where?"

"Right in the valley below the rocks at Dargill Creek. I didn't dare get closer," Joe said shifting from one leg to another. "But maybe you could go to see what this is all about."

"Sure. I will. I wanted to inspect the cattle there anyhow. Orville, are you game for a couple of hours in the saddle?"

Orville smiled. It was a challenge he couldn't refuse. "Of course. Let's go."

Elliott told Frank to load the wagon with hay and follow them to the pasture. He made a detour to the kitchen to tell Celestine where they were going and to take some bread, cheese, and cold beef if they were delayed on the range. Four Fingers was instructed to stay with Celestine and Annabelle to guard them.

They rode for a while without talking. Then, Orville bent his head backwards and whistled. "I see now what you mean. There is one thing to admire all this vastness from the wagon seat and another to ride free. It's a primitive feeling of being wild and unrestrained."

"And your own boss," Elliott added, thinking of the years he'd worked in a bank.

"Of course, then the reality catches up with you, greedy neighbors like Crawford, the cattle need feed, a blizzard from time to time. I'm aware it's not easy. But you get to experience this feeling of freedom every day."

"Yeah, I still do after five years. But think also of all the weird things I have to deal with, like this animal shot with an arrow."

"Indians?"

"Of course not. It's 1887. Someone wants to scare us," Elliott explained. "It has something to do with

Dargill Creek, a haunted place where legend says an old French trapper was ambushed and killed and he cursed the place. Many people who dared to go there spoke of ghosts haunting and that the spirit of the dead can't find peace and wails at night."

"Scary, indeed. Is that where we are going?" Orville asked.

"Yes. But not the way we were sent."

Orville slowed down his horse and looked at his brother. "What do you mean?"

"The valley below the rocks that border the creek on my side of property is the perfect place for an ambush. It's like a bucket where you have no place to hide except behind your horse."

"But Joe said that's where the animal was killed."

Elliott looked away. "That's what he said. I know Joe. While he was talking, his left eye ran sideways for a fraction of a second and back, like he was checking to see to the side. He was lying or hiding something."

"Your own man is sending you to an ambush?"

"I'm not sure, but I'm going to be cautious.

Usually I am or I wouldn't have survived here."

Orville pulled his hat lower on his face. "Do you think he's in cahoots with Crawford?"

"Perhaps, but not in this. Dargill Creek is a remote area to the northeast. The creek which runs into a ravine is the border between my land and Parker's. Crawford land is to the west, farther away, bordering Richardson's. I don't see Crawford crossing my land to go east or worse, detouring all the way through the wild terrain northeast of here," Elliott explained.

"Now you got me confused. Do you have more enemies than Crawford?"

"I thought not, but I can't be sure. We'll see." Elliott stopped talking. It crossed his mind that maybe his brother, living in a sheltered world all his life might not be eager to get into danger for a brother he was never close to. Old insecurities assaulted him. "Look, maybe I made a mistake assuming you wanted to ride out there with me. Facing all sorts of dangers is everyday life for me, but perhaps you don't wish to jump into a risky situation like this."

"Are you joking? I wouldn't miss it for the world. Lead on." Orville smiled at him.

They rode farther until they reached a gap in the fence. Elliott pointed to Orville. "We cross on Parker's land here and we make a detour and come on the other side of Dargill Creek. We'll have to leave the horses there and climb up the ravine to surprise whoever is hiding behind the rocks."

They tied the horses to a scrawny bush and descended in the ravine from the east side.

"You seem to know your way around here, cursed place or not," Orville observed, using his rifle as a stick to ease his descent.

Elliott grinned at him. "After I bought the land, I explored every corner and beyond. Four Fingers was my guide. He saved my life many times and taught me ranching. I've been here too, although there are some hidden caves that Four Fingers was too superstitious to explore. He said the spirits of the dead are still here and we should leave them alone."

At the bottom of the ravine, a gunmetal creek was

running, despite the below freezing temperature.

Orville shivered. "I see what he meant. It is a creepy place. I'm not superstitious, but I can feel the bad, almost hostile spirits."

"Like in a cemetery at night."

"Not all spirits in a cemetery are bad. Here they are. They make you feel like you are trespassing on forbidden grounds."

Elliott signaled they should be quiet now and they started to climb up the ravine on the steeper side toward the rocks. They were lucky Elliott knew the way or they wouldn't have made it.

When they were up among the rocks, Elliott pointed out a man, dressed in Indian garb, with a bow on the ground near him. He was watching the valley bellow. Elliott advanced careful not to make noise, but the silence was so eerie and ominous that every little sound was carried through the frigid air.

The man heard him and reached for the bow. Orville shot it out of his hand. At the sight of the broken bow, dismay showed on his face adorned with war paint.

He touched his gun tucked in the wide belt at his waist.

"Don't," Elliott advised him. "Your game is over."

The man rolled on the ground suddenly and disappeared from sight.

"How did he do that?" Orville asked amazed.

"Remember I told you there is a cave here," Elliott answered, studying the narrow space between two rocks.

"Are we going after him?"

"In the cave? No, we're not. If the passage narrows and we have to crawl, he can gun us down one at a time."

"You're not going to let him escape, are you?"

"No. I learned a little Indian trick. Let's see if it works."

Elliott gathered dry twigs from the bushes and dry grass and started a fire at the cave's entrance. After a few minutes, a man rushed out coughing, firing his gun wildly through the entrance. Elliott stepped aside and then behind him and stuck his rifle between his shoulder blades.

"Bring me the rope, Orville," he said. "We have another Christmas gift for the sheriff."

He was tying the man's hands behind his back when a well-known voice surprised them. "Are you still watching, Ephraim?"

"Shoot them, Joe," the man shouted, fighting to get free.

Orville coshed him on the head with the butt of his rifle. The man called Ephraim fell to the ground.

Joe's youthful face came on top of a big boulder.

Elliott hauled him up. "Now, explain to us how you came to know this person?"

Joe looked at Ephraim's body, sprawled on the ground, his hands tied, and his face crumpled. "He is my older brother. We grew up at an orphanage in St. Louis."

"Was he the one who suggested an ambush? Or was it your idea to send us into a trap in the valley bellow?"

"Look, he is my brother. He has always looked out for me and protected me from bigger boys. I respect you, Boss, but he's my brother," Joe said defiantly.

"When I found you starving at the train depot last summer, you said you'll do everything I ask. I suppose that was an empty promise. Or you were plotting with your brother even then," Elliott asked.

"No, no I didn't. He came to me only three weeks ago to tell me he had hired to Crawford. He had no choice, you see. He owed Crawford a lot of money from playing poker. The other man you caught several days ago, told me that they will kill Ephraim if I don't help them."

"You gave him a knife to cut his restraints on the drive to town. He almost escaped from the wagon. He wanted to kill us also."

"I had to, don't you understand? Ephraim is all the family I have," Joe looked at Elliott beseechingly.

"If you were so eager to help them, then why did they beat you within an inch of your life in front of the saloon?"

"I had not agreed to help them. The beating was to persuade me that they were serious about killing me and Ephraim."

Elliott looked at the valley below and beyond at his land. He was not joking when he told Orville that he would die protecting what was his and his rights.

"Boss, listen, I know you have no reason to trust me now, but I didn't help them willingly and Crawford will come to burn everything down if you don't sign the land over to him. You don't have many men. Let me prove myself. Let me help."

No. Even if he wanted to give him a chance, the risk of a second betrayal was too great. This was the law of the west. You were given a chance, but no one would look at you twice if you proved to be a traitor.

Elliott shook his head. "No. I will let you go free, because plotting with the enemy is not going to impress the sheriff as a big crime, but your brother is going to jail. He is the last gang member who robbed the train and ran away. I guess he thought to hide in this remote area under the Indian guise, hoping the sheriff will lose his track."

CHAPTER 21

While Elliott and Orville were riding to Dargill Creek, Celestine was playing with Annabelle and the little dog under the Christmas tree. She felt melancholic because the celebration was over and sad for having to dismantle the decorated tree that had brought so much joy in the dreary winter days.

She felt bereft of a purpose. Then she remembered that her father liked to eat shepherd's pie the day after Christmas. The cook made it from some of the leftovers. She would do the same. And bread pudding. What could be more delicious?

Animated by new energy, Celestine placed on the table what she needed for the savory pie. She stopped humming a carol when she heard the noise of approaching horses. She placed her old jacket over her shoulders, grabbed the rifle from the mantel, and went out on the porch. It was a wagon with two men on the seat coming at high speed. When it stopped in front of the house, she saw the driver was Tommy, the young clerk from the train depot.

Four Fingers came out of the barn as well to see who it was. He nodded slightly, confirming that there was no danger and went back inside.

The other man's face was not visible under the blankets piled on him and the scarves wrapped around his head. He was moaning and complaining about the frigid weather, the uncomfortable transportation, and life in general that had brought him to such wild place, far from civilization.

"Hey Tommy, who is your unhappy companion?" Celestine asked, laughing.

"I don't know him, Miss Celestine. But you should. He claims to be your fiancé," Tommy said jumping down from the seat.

"My fiancé?" That man burrowed under a coarse blanket, with his head covered by a plain scarf couldn't be Richard, who was always elegant and dandy, in his latest fashion suits and twirling his walking stick.

"Yes, ma'am. That's what he said. He paid me good money to bring him here, and I did, but I told him that he can't be your fiancé. Our Miss Celestine is going to marry rancher Maitland. Every one in town knows that. They are waiting to see you in church as a bride."

"Every one in town?" Celestine asked surprised.

"Yes, ma'am." Tommy bobbed his head up and down. "They'd be mighty disappointed if you didn't."

Celestine looked at Richard, who slid down from the tall wagon seat and looked upset by the slush adorning his shoes and pants.

"You, boy, unload my luggage and carry it inside," he ordered in a nasal voice and sneezed so loudly that the horses shied sideways.

"No way. Don't do it, Tommy. He's going right back where he came from. Regardless of my marital prospects, they don't involve him. I promise you that. Now come in to warm up with hot coffee and cookies before returning back to town."

"Thank you, I will." Tommy followed Celestine inside, cheered by the warmth radiated by the fireplace and the stove. Grumbling Richard came in after him.

After sipping the warm liquid in silence, Tommy

smacked his forehead with his hand. "I forgot that a letter came for you Miss Celestine, and as I drove this gent here I thought to give you the letter."

"You should have given it to me," Richard protested, revived from his stupor by the strong hot coffee.

"You're not Celestine Tillman, are you? See, it says here the addressee's name. As postal clerks, we have to be careful with these details." And with a flourished gesture Tommy handed Celestine the letter.

She looked at it briefly. It was from the same lawyer, Humphrey Dunn, Attorney-at-Law. Better to be read in private, and to Tommy's disappointment, she placed it in her skirt's pocket.

It seemed that the letter animated Richard. He looked around and with a dramatic gesture said, "Darling, I had no idea you lived here in such primitive conditions or I'd have come earlier."

Celestine looked at him like he'd just landed from the moon. "Really? This is a wonderful homestead. It doesn't look grand like the mansions in the east, but it offers all the comfort and warmth I needed when I was without shelter. It is much better than the place where I lived in Philadelphia. Remember? After I was evicted from my family home. No one came to my rescue then. Certainly not you."

"It was a misunderstanding…"

"No, it was very clear to me when you sent your man to ask for the return of your engagement ring. Remember?" she repeated. "You said the engagement was off. And so it is, and it stays off."

Richard sputtered, "I had to do it. Think of my position in society."

"Are you talking about your position as inveterate gambler? Or about the fact that you owed a lot of money to half the town?"

He opened his mouth, then snapped it shut. The Celestine he remembered had been more compliant and biddable than this shrew who argued with him openly. If he didn't need money desperately, he wouldn't be here at the end of the world trying to convince her of his love.

Tommy was looking from one to the other

fascinated. Now, things were getting interesting and he had what to tell people in town. Besides, Miss Celestine was spoken to Maitland anyone knew that, not because the town talked, but it was enough to look at them making moony eyes at each other. It was clear that love was in the air.

"Darling," Richard tried again after taking a deep breath. "You know how it was. Your father was a compromised figure in town. His bank was not solvent and his partner ran off with the money."

"My father was the most honest man in all Philadelphia," Celestine protested, struggling with the strong emotions she felt.

"Yes, well, we know this now. But almost a year ago the evidence was against him."

A warning bell rang in Celestine's mind. "What do you mean, 'we know this now'?" she asked.

Richard waved his hand. "You'll find out from that lawyer's letter. The police in New York caught up with the partner when he tried to board on a ship due to sail to England. They found all the money on him. Your father was declared innocent. So you see, darling there is no reason not to return to Philadelphia with me."

"On the contrary, I see no reason to return with you."

In all this time, Annabelle had listened quietly, frowning from time to time. She didn't understand much of what the grown-up people were talking about, but she felt that the stranger wanted to take Celestine away. Annabelle didn't like that at all. Celestine belonged with Uncle Elliott and she discovered that she liked having a larger family. This place where Uncle Elliott lived was full of surprises and adventure. Who needed California? Well, her mother did, but Annabelle was sure her mother would understand that it was better for them to remain here.

Richard continued his argument. "Surely you don't intend to live here among these uncouth people."

"Hey, see here mister, I don't know where you come from, but we in Wyoming Territory are fine people. We may get drunk at the saloon on Saturday nights, but what man doesn't?" Tommy protested hurt in his pride of the locals.

Richard ignored him. "You belong to the most refined society in Philadelphia. You don't mean to live here. Look around you. This is…"

Annabelle, who had come closer, blinked innocently. "…pretty. This house is pretty," she said and stuck her thumb into her mouth.

Other children her age did this as a sign they were confused, even scared. With Annabelle, this gesture signaled that she had a mischievous plan in the works. Celestine knew this and looked at her with suspicion. What had the spirited child done now? But Annabelle seemed concerned only by the heated discussion between the adults in the room.

It was time to put an end to all this. Celestine had no idea what expectations Richard had of her. She was not president of a bank to loan him money. Whatever it was he wanted, he was not going to get it.

She rose and the rules of politeness demanded that the men present had to be standing too. "Tommy, I'll wrap some cookies for you to have on your way and please take this gentleman with you to the train depot. He should not miss the next train going east."

Richard said stubbornly, "No, I'm not going without you."

He must have been more desperate for money than she thought. Just when she was wondering how to make him leave before Elliott came home and had him forcibly removed, the door burst open and Four Fingers came in with a scary scowl on his face. He waved a big knife in one hand and had an axe in the other. And was that a turkey feather drooping from his hair? "Ha, ha," he yelled at Richard.

"Help!" Richard cried and circling the table, ran out the door to the wagon still waiting there. The back of his overcoat was covered in a whitish residue.

Tommy patted the Indian on the back. "Well done, Four Fingers. I thought he would never leave."

Celestine smiled at them. "Thank you both. Although the axe was overkill."

"I have to go," Tommy announced. "I'll see that he's in the first train due east." He turned back at the door. "By the way, what was that white stain on his back?"

Celestine thought about it and turned to Annabelle. "Do you know, young lady?"

The little girl nodded. "It was flour from that sack." She pointed to a burlap sack near the stove. "His coat was wet so it stuck."

"I bet it stuck. Water and flour, I bet it is glue by now," Tommy observed. "It will take me a long time to clean my wagon seat."

"Not as long as it will take him to clean his coat," Four Fingers observed dryly.

But Annabelle returned to the tree where the little dog snored undisturbed, and started to rock her doll, singing an off-key lullaby. She was the perfect picture of a well-behaved little girl.

CHAPTER 22

Joe had left the previous evening without talking to any of the ranch hands. He had tried to return the book to Celestine.

"I'm sorry, Miss Celestine," he said sadly. "I guess I'll always be a dumb cowboy, who doesn't know to read."

"Don't give up, Joe. You're a good man. Don't let evil forces drag you to their side. Don't forget that it's never too late to learn to read and to improve yourself. As for the book, it's yours. A Christmas gift can't be taken back."

"Thank you, ma'am. I'll treasure it always." He mounted his horse and rode away.

"I hope he doesn't ride straight to Crawford," Elliott said, coming out on the porch near her to look at the departing rider. "Or worse; I hope he doesn't try to bust his brother out of jail where we will be taking him tomorrow."

"No, he won't. Joe is a good man. He is confused

and torn between loyalty to his older brother and what his conscience tells him is right," Celestine explained.

"That remains to be seen," Elliott concluded, guiding her inside. He had his doubts about Joe. It was a lesson he had learned in his hard life. People could not be trusted. How could Celestine believe the good would prevail, considering everything she had endured after her father's death?

Next day, Elliott and Orville had to take the train robber to the sheriff.

"Shall I bring the wagon?" Orville asked.

"No, the wagon will slow us down. We'll ride."

Easier said than done. The robber was kicking and trying to pull away, until Elliott told him, "You can mount in the saddle on your own, or we can throw you there, in which case you'll ride all the way to town face down on the horse's back. Your choice."

That convinced the robber and he mounted without protest.

Elliott stepped up on the porch to say good-bye to

Celestine. He touched her cheek and he marveled at the velvety soft skin and her luminous golden-brown eyes. Peaches and cream cheeks. How on earth had he thought of her as a prune when he had seen her for the first time in Sam's mercantile?

"I'm going to town, Celestine. Tell me what you'd like me to bring you from there," he asked, knowing women liked trinkets, and thinking this would make her happy. How else could a man court a woman and show his appreciation?

"You. Bring yourself back safe," she answered smiling.

Elliott nodded and kissed her on the mouth right there in full view of his cheering cowboys and of his grinning brother. He had accepted that Celestine was very precious to him, despite knowing her for such a short time. This was the west after all. Life went by at a faster pace and a man had to make up his mind fast or another man would grab the opportunity. And Elliott had already decided to ask Celestine to marry him that evening when he returned from town.

"Stop grinning like a fool," he told his brother, while climbing in the saddle. They were comfortable enough with each other now to exchange teasing remarks. He grabbed the bridle of the horse with the robber, who had his hands tied together and to the pommel. Orville rode behind them keeping an eye on the robber, with his rifle ready.

They rode quickly and in a little more than an hour the first buildings of Laramie came into view. Elliott breathed more easily. He had feared that they would be attacked on the way to town. Probably Crawford didn't value Ephraim as much as Joe did.

They stopped in front of the sheriff's office. Elliott looked around and told Orville, "Wait here, and keep an eye on him."

He entered the office, where he found only Young Jeremiah, drinking coffee and lazing in the chair behind the desk. He was too young, as the name said, to be a deputy sheriff, but unfortunately there were no other choices, so he was doing the best he could.

"Where's the sheriff?" Elliott asked him.

"He rode shotgun on the stagecoach to Centennial. He had some inquiry to make at the mining camp there. He'll be back in the evening."

Elliott took his hat off and slapped it against his thigh. Darn, his bad luck. "There is no choice then. Jeremiah, you'll have to help me. I have an outlaw with me. Between my brother and me, we can drag him into one of the jail cells and lock him up. He's not cooperative, but we'll manage."

"Yes, sir. Mr. Maitland. Here are the keys," Jeremiah answered, properly impressed by anyone catching an outlaw.

Elliott rolled his eyes. The young man was full of good intentions, but naïve. Any man with a good story could coax the jail keys out of him. "You see, the problem isn't to get him behind bars, but to keep him there. There are people willing to do whatever it takes to get him out. Do you understand?"

"Yes, sir. Absolutely."

"Nobody should get those keys. Hide them and pretend you don't have them."

Jeremiah nodded. "Yes, sir. I'll throw them in the spittoon right now."

Elliott grabbed his hand. "Not right now. We have to lock him inside first."

"Ah, yes." Jeremiah looked at Elliott in awe. "I wish I were as smart as you Mr. Maitland."

"Well, when he'll be back, just tell the sheriff that we caught the wanted man in the poster."

"The wanted man. Wait." Jeremiah pulled a bunch of Wanted posters out of the top drawer. "Which one?"

Elliott leafed through them. It didn't take him long to find the face with a sadistic glint in his eyes. Yep, he'd been right. No mistake. That was the man. "This one."

"And you have him outside?"

"Yes. Or I hope he's still there after having this long talk with you," Elliott added impatiently.

Young Jeremiah scratched his head. "If he's wanted like it says here, for murdering a bank clerk during a robbery in Kansas and killing a man in a saloon in Colorado, then we should take him to the Territorial Prison."

"We can't. He has not been convicted of any crime yet. He needs to stay in jail until then."

"Yes, it's true. But I know for sure that there is a marshal there today for a transfer of prisoners. He'll leave tomorrow, but if your man is a wanted killer I think we could get him interested to watch over him perhaps even until the trial. As for the prison, many times when we have a wanted outlaw, the sheriff doesn't want him together with just drunkards or disorderly people. So we ask the prison guards to keep him there."

It was an idea. Not a bad one and it might work. "Bring the poster with you and lock the office," Elliott ordered him. He had to catch the marshal. Otherwise, he doubted the prison people in charge would listen to Jeremiah.

Outside, he found a few curious onlookers that had gathered, but no one aggressive. He mounted his horse and pulled the outlaw's horse after him. Orville followed behind with his rifle in one hand.

Luck was with them at the Territorial Prison. The marshal was still there. When presented with the poster, he was eager to make sure the outlaw was secured behind bars and he was happy to do it.

"You have no idea how long we have been chasing this man. What's written here…" He pointed to the poster. "…that is only a few of his crimes. He looks young, but so did Billy the Kid. He is ruthless. He shot a whole farming family in Nebraska just because he wanted their horse. He savaged a girl working in a saloon in Colorado because she dropped whisky on his coat. I will make it my personal mission to see that he stays here until the trial. I'm glad you caught him alive. Killing him would have been an easy escape from his crimes. Your sheriff will pay you the reward money. We'll send it to him in a week or so. Good job."

Well, one problem was solved, and he had another more pleasant task before returning home. Elliott pulled out of his pocket the watch Celestine had given him. It was working well and he had gotten into the habit of checking the time.

They stopped their horses in front of Trabing store. He knew exactly what he wanted.

"You're going to buy a ring," Orville guessed.

"No. I'm going to give her Mama's garnet ring, but I want to buy her garnet earrings," Elliott answered, pushing the entrance door open.

He explained to the clerk what he wanted. After trying to sell him ruby earrings, the clerk pulled out of a cabinet a splendid pair, with garnets glittering in the electric lights newly installed in the store.

"Perfect." Elliott breathed and paid cash, while the clerk packaged the earrings in a dark blue velvet box. He had credit at Sam's mercantile, but preferred to pay cash when he was shopping here occasionally.

He placed the package in his pocket and they went out the store, ready to return home.

Across the street, there was a land recording office and a lawyer's business. He saw Emory Miller coming out with another younger man. They shook hands and went in opposite directions.

"Wait here," he told Orville and sprinted across

the street to catch up with Miller.

"Hey, Miller," he called.

The older rancher turned and faced him.

"Maitland." He inclined his head.

"Look, you can tell me it's none of my business, and you'd be right, but the stakes are too high to ignore what is going on. Did you sell to Crawford?"

Miller looked at him with sadness and sighed.

"No, not to Crawford. But I had to sell, Maitland. I'm too old to keep fighting alone. None of my children are interested in working the land. I sold the ranch to a young fellow called John Gorman. He offered me a decent price, about four times more than Crawford's paltry offer. I'd have been crazy not to take it."

"So, what are you going to do now?"

"The ranch was my home and I had hoped to make it a prosperous place. But I have to adapt. I'm not sure where I'll end up. My brother-in-law has a shoemaking business in Providence, Rhode Island. I could buy into his business. This would be my safest option. Or I could go to Colorado to join my sons in prospecting for gold. I still have a sense of adventure left in me. I don't know."

Elliott nodded. "Well, good luck whatever you decide to do. Thank you for not selling to Crawford." They shook hands and Elliott returned to where he'd left his brother.

On the boardwalk, an Indian was waving back and forth muttering some weird words to himself. When Elliott walked by, he almost fell into his path.

He looked down and in a low voice heard only by Elliott he said, "They'll come tonight. Be ready." Then he continued to mutter his gibberish.

Elliott bent too and whispered back through clenched teeth. "Thank you for the warning, Bold Eagle." Then he pushed him away and said in a loud voice, "Watch out, fellow."

The brothers climbed in the saddle and rode away.

Behind them, the Indian man continued to wave and chant in a low voice.

CHAPTER 23

They rode toward the ranch in silence. They had to talk, but not now on the road. Elliott had been looking forward to proposing to Celestine and to having a quiet night at home. Now, under the threat of Crawford attacking them, he had to postpone his proposal.

It was almost dark when they dismounted at home. Celestine was on the porch and Elliott hugged her to him, burying his face in her sweet smelling hair. No words, not yet. She felt his dark mood and didn't ask any questions.

Elliott waited until his ranch hands, fewer now with Joe gone, were all seated around the table.

"In these past few days, Crawford's threat has increased. He hired men, including a famous gunslinger, and it is possible he'll attack us tonight. It's not fair, but life seldom is, and a man needs to stand up and fight for what is his. However, this is my fight, not yours. I don't know how it will end. It is dangerous and you all don't have to place your life in danger for a fight that is not yours. I've decided to give you the choice to stay and fight with me or to simply go away and be safe. If you choose to go, that is your choice. I understand. No hard feelings. You're free to go."

His somber mood had spread to the others.

"I can't believe no one will help us." Frank finally broke the silence.

"Parker might. But he has children and I can't ask him to place his life in danger for me."

"You just returned from town. What about the sheriff?"

"The sheriff is gone with the stagecoach to Centennial. He will be back tonight, but it's too late. So I have to fight this alone as I always did. Frank, what's your decision?"

"I'll stay, of course. You gave me a job when no one else would look at me, the son of the town's drunkard. You were fair and we ate at the same table. I spent Christmas here and I got my first personal gift." He touched the red scarf at his neck. "The money you gave us was great, but this is special."

"All right. Thank you for staying," Elliott said, turning to his left. "Pirate, what about you?"

The Pirate looked down, twirling his curled moustache. "You all know that I'm not much of a fighter. Gambling is my specialty. I figure I'll head to town and be back later."

Frank jumped up from his chair. "Are you abandoning us? Don't bother to come back. You're not much of a worker either."

The Pirate narrowed his eyes. Elliott raised his hand to calm them down. "He's free to go, Frank. Don't forget I promised no resentment towards those who leave." The Pirate placed his hat on, bowed politely to Celestine and quietly left the house.

Elliott turned to Four Fingers. "How about you old friend? You helped me countless times, but this fight is bound to be bloody and I'm not going to beat around the bush. We might all be dead by morning."

"You don't need to ask me, Maitland. I was here before you and my name may not be on that piece of paper you call deed, but I've lived and worked on this land. This is my home. Where would I go?" Four Fingers answered.

Elliott touched his hand. "Thank you... Orville, I dread having to ask you, but I have to. Are you going to stay or leave?"

"Are you kidding? I said I'd stay at least until this dangerous situation with Crawford is resolved."

"I am grateful to have you beside me, but you have to think of Annabelle. Maybe you should leave for her sake."

Orville shook his head. "I thought of her and of this new life I'm trying to make for her here out west. There are dangers everywhere. We'll hide her in the cellar until the fight is over."

Celestine smiled at him reassuringly. "I'll take care of her, Orville. I'll protect her with my life."

Elliott intervened. "We all know how resourceful you are Celestine. But keep in mind that Crawford's henchmen are professional fighters and they are coming intent to kill us all."

"Maybe only intent to burn the buildings to the

ground and to scare you into selling," Four Fingers corrected him calmly.

"Elliott, you know I'm not a sheltered woman. I can fight and shoot like any man. You asked me before and my answer is the same. I'm staying."

"Very well, then. Let's eat quickly and drink a lot of coffee. We'll not have much sleep tonight. Then we'll spread out. We'll leave the bunkhouse empty. Frank and Four Fingers you should stay in the barn to protect the animals. The barn loft is a perfect place for observation and has the advantage of being high. You can surprise them from above. Orville and I will defend the house. Take some buckets of water with you, just in case it catches fire."

They ate fast and then the men left to take their positions in the barn.

Elliott showed Orville a hidden space behind the fireplace, between two stone walls, that was protected from the fire. "Annabelle will be safe here and warm from the fireplace."

"How did you discover this place?"

"I stumbled into the wall here, trying to see if the flue was open."

Quietly, Celestine loaded two rifles and placed the bullets box handy.

Elliott shook his head. "You are going into the hiding place with Annabelle, ma'am."

"No, I'm not. I can shoot better than most men. My aim is accurate." She raised her chin in protest.

"Celestine, come here." He took her by the waist and pulled her close to him. "I couldn't bear it if anything happened to you. Do you understand? You are my weakness. Let me have the peace of mind that you are safe."

She looked at him with her soft golden eyes. "I can't do this, Elliott. Because this goes both ways. I couldn't stay hidden there knowing that you are in danger. Let me help. The settlers coming west had families to support them. They stood together and fought together."

Reluctantly, Elliott closed the door to the hidden place on a sleeping Annabelle. "I don't know what will happen tomorrow, but I want you to know that in the short time since I've met you, I've come to admire you. I'm not good with words. I love you, Celestine. Truly, honestly. I'll tell you more tomorrow if I'll be alive. Until then, please wear this." Elliott placed his mother's garnet ring on her slender finger. "It was my mother's."

Celestine looked at the ring, then raised her eyes to him. "Elliott…"

"Shh, no more words." He kissed her finger and, pulling her closer, kissed her mouth with passion, disheartened to think it might be for the last time.

"Riders are coming," Orville announced, after receiving the signal from Frank in the loft.

"Don't shoot. I have to see what they want," Elliott ordered.

"Like you don't know already," Orville muttered.

The night sky was clear and the moon was lighting up the high plains of Laramie. On any other night, Elliott would stop to marvel yet again at the majestic starry sky. Not tonight. The riders were armed and carrying torches, certainly not to light their path.

Elliott stepped out on the porch and fired a warning shot in front of the advancing men. "Stop right there. State your business and go."

Crawford, mounted on his nervous stallion, came forward. "I am a generous man, Maitland. I thought I'd give you a chance to sign the property over to me and leave unharmed. This is your last chance."

"I told you before, my land is not for sale. I'll die protecting it."

"You just might, Maitland," Crawford answered, laughing maliciously. His men echoed his laugh and one of them turned his hand, preparing to throw the torch to the barn.

A shot rang in the night. With a cry, the hired man dropped the torch and reached for his gun. This time the second shot threw him off his horse to the icy ground. The attackers jumped off their horses taking positions behind the wagon, the horses' trough, various barrels, and other objects spread in the yard. They were all grumbling, unhappy for not being able to surprise their intended victim.

They started shooting at random at the barn and at the house. Elliott dropped down on the porch and returned fire.

He saw two men crawling on the ground behind the barn.

"Orville, cover me," he shouted to his brother. From the window, Orville fired in the yard repetitively. Elliott ran and circled the barn. He surprised the two men just when they were trying to set fire to the side of the barn and the wet grass nearby.

"Hands up and don't move," he shouted. One of them reached for his gun and Elliott fired. He collapsed on the ground taking with him the torch that continued to burn slowly on the icy ground turning it into slush.

Elliott directed his rifle toward the other one, just when he was inching his hand downward to grab his gun. Elliott fired in front of him. "Don't try or I'll kill you."

"You don't have the guts to do it, boy."

Ah, just his luck to catch Crawford in the act of setting fire to his barn. "I shot your hireling, didn't I?

The reason I don't want to kill you is because I want to see you punished for killing my cattle, poisoning Miller's bull, sending men to beat my ranch hands, and threatening my people."

"You'll never prove it was me."

"Of course, I will. We have a sheriff who is not easily intimidated by the likes of you."

Crawford looked beyond Elliott's shoulder and his face lit up with relief. Elliott kept his attention and rifle on him. At first, he thought that Crawford may be trying to distract him, but then he heard a horse's trot coming near.

"Kill him, Joe. We'll pop your brother out of jail and I'll make you foreman on this ranch," Crawford told the newcomer.

Elliott could have told him that if he was shot, then his finger would press the trigger and Crawford would be shot too. But the voice behind him answered first.

"I'm no killer like my brother, Crawford. It took me all night to understand that two men can be raised in the same place and then go in different directions in life. I love my brother, but I'm not responsible for his actions."

"Then your brother will rot in jail."

"He deserves to rot for the crimes he committed. I want no part of this." Joe turned his horse and rode away.

CHAPTER 24

Celestine's voice rang clear above the noise of guns in the yard. "I'll kill you all if you've harmed Elliott. You have no right to come here." A volley of rifle bullets followed her words.

"Ah, the spirited Miss Tillman. She's still with you, I suppose. Where would she go and who would want her?" Crawford said, trying to provoke Elliott's ire and distract him.

"You forget she beat three of your men and chased you away with only a Derringer. Imagine what she can do with a rifle. Every single man in town wants her, but she's mine. Now enough talking." Elliott wished he had a rope handy, but there was none here, outside the barn.

Again, the noise of a horse's trot sounded, and this time Elliott did try to look over his shoulder. A second was all it took and Crawford pulled his gun out of the holster. Elliott fired his rifle a second too late. The newcomer shot Crawford and he fell to the ground, clutching his chest.

Elliott took Crawford's gun away and the knife in his belt. He was in no condition to fight again, but Elliott wanted to be sure. Then he turned to the newcomer. The rider was young, blond and blue-eyed, and a complete stranger.

"I don't know who you are and why you are here in the middle of the night, but I'm grateful to you. You saved my life. Thank you." Elliott eyed him with interest.

The stranger leaned forward over the pommel of his saddle, his Colt still in his hand. "I was riding in the neighborhood when I saw all these gents riding across the field with torches. The chances that they were a religious procession were minimal. Having a curious nature, I followed them here. I don't like people who have fun burning barns and houses." He straightened, looking across the yard. "Ah, the sheriff is here. I'll be going then."

"Wait!" Elliott stopped him. "Who are you?"

"John Gorman is my name," he answered, then saluted and rode away.

The name was not unfamiliar to Elliott, but he couldn't remember where he'd heard it. He hauled Crawford's body up and despite the loud moaning, he carried and dragged him to the front yard.

Indeed the sheriff was there and was rounding up Crawford's men. "Maitland, I heard you had a busy night," the sheriff said, hauling another protesting man into the wagon, his hands tied. "Frank, tie their feet too like you do with the steers," he said.

"Here, Sheriff, this is Crawford. I caught him just when he was trying to set fire to my barn with a torch. They came prepared." Elliott pushed his enemy into the wagon.

"Who winged him?" the sheriff wanted to know.

"A fellow I've never seen before. John Gorman." A spark of recognition came to his mind when he heard the name. "Miller just sold his ranch to him."

The sheriff nodded, continuing his task securing his prisoners. "I've heard."

"How did you know to come here in the middle of the night?" Elliott asked the sheriff.

"Your man, the Pirate, alerted me."

Elliott saw the Pirate near the corral, mounted on his horse, looking in the darkness. He approached him. "Thank you for bringing the sheriff. This stopped the fight before it caused more bloodshed. You can come back to work anytime you want."

"I appreciate the offer, but I am not a good cowboy. Gambling is more my style. I'll be heading west to Nevada. Virginia City is not as rich as ten years ago, the mines are almost abandoned, but there are some saloons good for gamblers like me."

"Good luck," Elliott said and extended his hand. They shook hands and the Pirate galloped away.

Elliott looked around. On the porch, Celestine was looking at him, rifle still in her hands. He opened his arms and she dropped the rifle and flew to him, nestling at his chest.

"We heard gun shots on the other side of the barn where you were and we couldn't see. I thought you were wounded or worse," she blurted, her voice filled both with the fear she felt for him and relief to see him unharmed.

Elliott looked up at the barn's loft window where Four Fingers nodded that he was all right. He'd seen Frank helping the sheriff and his brother on the porch, unharmed also. "Nobody was hurt," he said with satisfaction.

Orville came running from the house, a desperate look in his eyes. "Annabelle has vanished. She's not in the hiding place. What if someone kidnapped her?"

"Knowing Annabelle, it's more likely that she woke up and wandered outside," Elliott tried to reason with his brother, although he was worried. If the mischievous child had gone far at this hour of the night, she could get into danger.

Attracted by their cries, the sheriff ordered Frank to guard the wagon and went to search with them.

"You see the door to the hideout is open. She left on her own. There was no outlaw riding away and we didn't see her outside," Elliott said.

"She was not in the front yard either or we'd have seen her," Celestine mentioned. "She must have gotten out through one of the back windows." She ran to the parlor and there they found the window open.

The sheriff went outside. Under the window, he found tiny footprints going down to the creek behind the house. Elliott and Orville rushed out to join him.

"She must have gone to the creek," Elliott observed.

The sheriff raised a finger to his mouth to silence them. Carried by the breeze, a childish voice piped into the night.

"I could shoot you, 'boom, boom' and you could pretend you're dead."

"Ay, that gun is not a toy for a little girl like you. Give it to me," a man's voice said.

"No, don't come any closer." A cracking sound accompanied the girl's voice.

"Are you crazy? You grazed my arm," the man said.

The sheriff reached the river first. In the moonlight, he saw a little girl with a Derringer in her hands several feet away from a man trying to get closer to her.

The sheriff pulled out his gun. "Hands up and don't move," he warned the outlaw.

"Don't come closer," Annabelle said and she fired the little pistol again.

"Drat," the sheriff said, grabbing his thigh.

"That's a bad word," Annabelle announced, turning back to the sheriff.

Orville intervened. "No, Annabelle, don't shoot. He is the sheriff."

"Papa." Annabelle dropped the Derringer in the snow and ran to her father.

Orville caught her in his arms. "I'm sorry, Sheriff. Are you wounded?"

"Only a scratch, but it hurts like…" He looked at Annabelle who was the picture of childish innocence in her father's arms. "It just hurts," he finished. "I'd appreciate it if you folks don't tell anyone about this. That would be the end of my days as sheriff," Bill Monroe added.

"What about the outlaw?"

"I think he fainted. I'd be obliged if you two would carry him to my wagon."

Elliott nodded and grabbed the outlaw by the arm. Orville handed Annabelle to Celestine and grabbed his other arm, which elicited a lugubrious moan from the man.

"We'll help you drive them to town. It is the right thing to do. Your jail will be crowded tonight, Sheriff."

"I'll take them to the Territorial Prison. A ruthless gang of outlaws running around my county, trying to kill people and stock and to burn their houses. Not one of them will escape from there. It's up to the judge after that."

CHAPTER 25

March, 1888, Laramie, Wyoming Territory

Celestine looked at the blue sky. Spring was finally coming. It was in the air. She planned to dig a vegetable garden as soon as the soil thawed. Elliott had warned her that they could have blizzards even in April. But she knew that once the soil thawed, every snowfall would just pass over, and after a few days, warm weather would follow. The growing season was short, but she intended to take advantage of it.

She'd been a married woman for almost three months and she couldn't be happier. How strange that she, raised in the luxurious world of high society Philadelphia, in a house full of modern amenities, was completely happy here in the wilds of Wyoming Territory.

"You see, Papa, I'm happy. I love Elliott and he loves me. He is a good man," she whispered looking up to the sky. "And I'm glad your good name was restored."

Or at least she hoped so. Richard wouldn't have come if he was not sure the opinion about her father had changed.

Philadelphia seemed so far away now.

Her eyes stopped on the horizon where a dot was growing larger and coming closer. A wagon. There was no more danger, but just in case, she went inside and grabbed the rifle. The men were on the range and she was home alone.

The wagon stopped in front of the house. It was Tommy, the young clerk from the train depot. She leaned the rifle against the wall and descended the porch steps. "Tommy, what did you bring me?" she asked, wiping her hands in her ruffled apron.

"Another gent who claims to know you, although this one isn't your fiancé."

A middle aged man, dressed in a fashionable suit, tried to clamber out of the wagon in a dignified way without much success.

"Come in, Tommy. I made fresh bread."

"Wow, yummy." Tommy inhaled the aroma from the kitchen.

The man stopped in front of her and bowed ceremoniously. "Miss Celestine Tillman?"

She smiled. "I'm Mrs. Maitland now."

"You got married?"

Her smile waned. "Yes, I did," she answered rather curtly, not liking the inquisitorial way he was questioning her.

"I'm Humphrey Dunn, Attorney-at-Law. I sent you a letter three months ago. Did you receive it?"

"Of course," Tommy answered in her stead. "I brought it to her personally."

Now she remembered. The day Richard had come, she had placed the letter in the pocket of her old skirt. So many things had happened after that, and she had forgotten the letter completely.

She poured coffee in china cups and sliced fresh bread and placed it on the table with butter and honey. She smiled demurely. "Maybe you could remind me what you wrote."

He paused and placed the coffee cup on the table. "Maybe I should talk to your husband," he said undecided.

Her tactic had backfired. Now he thought her an empty head female in need of a man's guidance. "Please tell me what it's all about. Here in the Wyoming Territory women have more rights, the right to vote and to stand in jury."

"Is that so? I've heard about it, but I couldn't believe it. What is the world coming to?" the lawyer wondered.

"Perhaps getting to real equal rights among all citizens," Celestine answered.

"Yes, well, in my letter, I was pleased to inform you that the police caught your father's partner and your father was completely absolved of any wrong doing. More than that, almost all the stolen money was found. The bank was reopened under the supervision of a board of trustees."

"I'm glad to hear it. My father would be happy. Of course, it's too late for him now," Celestine wiped a tear from the corner of her eyes.

"At least justice has been done and his partner

was indicted for his murder. It's probably difficult for you to grasp the reality, but you are the sole owner of the bank. Your father's personal fortune has been restored to you and it is worth almost a million dollars."

Hearing this, Tommy swallowed the wrong way and Celestine had to pat him on the back.

Satisfied with the strong effect of his words, the lawyer stood and picked up his suitcase. "I'll be at the hotel until tomorrow afternoon when my train is scheduled. I'll expect you and your husband there in the morning to sign some papers." He nodded to her and left.

Tommy followed him, but he turned back at the door and whispered to her. "Is it true Miss Celestine? Are you a millionaire?"

"No, Tommy," she assured him. "He was just funning."

"Ah, I thought so. Too good to be true." Whistling, Tommy climbed on the seat and turned the wagon around. Too bad he had no story to tell people in town.

Later that night when Celestine lay in her husband's arms, she said, "Guess what, Elliott? Your wife is a millionaire."

"Celestine, you ate sour cream again and Junior is acting up." He placed his hand gently on her stomach.

"What would you do if I had that much money?" she asked him.

"I'd keep it in a trust for our children. You forget that I have money now. We are rich. I just deposited five hundred dollars in my bank account from the reward I got for catching the bank robber."

* * *

Keep reading for a sneak peek of Old West Wyoming Book 2 - *The Train To Laramie*

The Train To

Laramie

VIVIAN SINCLAIR

CHAPTER 1

Laramie, Wyoming Territory, March 1888

With a screech of the iron wheels braking on the tracks, the train stopped at the depot releasing a huge cloud of white steam. The attendant opened the car doors, ready to help passengers to step down on the platform.

A handsome, well dressed gentleman, with a portmanteau in his hand stopped for a moment in the door, looking over the crowd. Then he descended with care the three tall steps before landing on the platform. Ignoring the attendant, he extended his hand to help the lady who waited in the doorway.

She was exquisitely beautiful, with blond curls, under a stylish hat adorned with velvet flowers and feathers. She had a doll-like face with porcelain skin, big blue eyes and a small upturned nose. She was dressed in an elegant outfit following the latest fashion. But what impressed most people looking at her was her air of indefinite melancholy and sadness.

She accepted the gentleman's hand and gracefully descended onto the platform. He bowed over her hand, kissed the tips of her gloved fingers, and turning away, left the depot walking in the general direction of Kuster Hotel.

The lady looked after him, sighed and turned around. She bumped into a tall man, who was making his way on the platform. With his round glasses, he looked like a fumbling, shy schoolteacher. Only at a second glance, the onlooker observed the steely determination in his grey-blue eyes and the star pinned on his shirt.

He grabbed her upper arms to steady her, then stepped back and touched his hat. "Pardon me, ma'am. I was looking elsewhere."

She nodded her understanding as she had been distracted too. Her eyes halted on his badge. "Isn't Bill Monroe our sheriff?"

"Yes, ma'am. He still is. I'm his deputy. Orville Maitland is my name."

A buggy coming at high speed, stopped in the

street right in front of the train depot. The driver, dressed in cowboy clothes, jumped down and sprinted through the passengers that were leaving the depot. When he saw the beautiful woman with a fancy hat, he breathed easier.

"I'm sorry I am late, Esmé." He kissed her cheek. Then he smiled at the deputy. "Orville, you've met my sister, Esmé, at the Christmas service in church."

"Yes, of course," the deputy answered politely, although for the life of him he couldn't remember her. Orville Maitland had met Lloyd Richardson, just before Christmas when Lloyd and Orville's brother, Elliott had caught the robbers that had stopped the train outside of town.

He raised his hat ready to go, when Lloyd, one arm protectively around his sister, stopped him. "Did you find your Wanted man?"

"No, I haven't seen him. Maybe he jumped off the train before it arrived at the depot. No one was robbed, so I'm not sure if he was in the train. He doesn't look like a common robber. He looks like a dandy, in both clothing and manners. Until he pulls a gun from his coat and relieves the travelers of their valuables."

"He needs to be caught, Orville. Innocent people like Esmé could be hurt." Lloyd Richardson slapped his hat to his thigh in frustration. "She travels often to Cheyenne and even Chicago. We have family there."

"Sheriff Monroe and I, we're doing the best we can to catch him. Sometimes we get a tip that he might be on the train, and it proves to be false. And we are fumbling in the dark if he looks like a regular passenger and not like your everyday outlaw," Orville explained.

None of them realized that Esmé was unusually quiet and frowning. She looked away at the street and back at her brother.

* * *

To find out about new releases and about other books written by Vivian Sinclair visit her website at VivianSinclairBooks.com or follow her on the Author page at Amazon, Facebook at Vivian Sinclair Books, or on GoodReads.com

Maitland Legacy, A Family Saga Trilogy - western contemporary fiction
Book 1 – Lost In Wyoming – Lance's story
Book 2 – Moon Over Laramie – Tristan's story
Book 3 – Christmas In Cheyenne – Raul's story

Wyoming Christmas Trilogy – western contemporary fiction
Book 1 – Footprints In The Snow – Tom's story
Book 2 – A Visitor For Christmas – Brianna's story
Book 3 – Trapped On The Mountain – Chris' story

Summer Days In Wyoming Trilogy - western contemporary fiction
Book 1 – A Ride In The Afternoon
Book 2 – Fire At Midnight
Book 3 – Misty Meadows At Dawn

Old West Wyoming - western historical fiction
Book 1 - A Western Christmas
Book 2 - The Train To Laramie
Book 3 - The Last Stage Coach

Seattle Rain series - women's fiction novels
Book 1 - A Walk In The Rain

Book 2 – Rain, Again!
Book 3 – After The Rain

Virginia Lovers Trilogy - contemporary romance:
Book 1 – Alexandra's Garden
Book 2 – Ariel's Summer Vacation
Book 3 – Lulu's Christmas Wish

A Guest At The Ranch – western contemporary romance

Storm In A Glass Of Water – a small town story

3 1333 04705 1923

Made in the USA
Lexington, KY
29 January 2018